Sinister Weapons

Hands that were so skillful in arousing her senses. Kisses that were so effective in stilling her fears. Words that were so cunning in quieting her doubts.

The Duke of Dacre used all of these weapons and so many more to conquer the young beauty who had become his unwilling bride.

But even when Christina could not keep herself from surrendering her body, she steeled her heart with a vow that she had not yet begun to fight....

A Difficult Truce

Dear Reader:

As you know, Signet is proud to keep bringing you the best in romance and now we're happy to announce that we are now presenting you with even more of what you love!

The Regency has long been one of the most popular settings for romances and it's easy to see why. It was an age of elegance and opulence, of wickedness and wit. It was also a time of tumultuous change, the beginning of the modern age and the end of illusion, when money began to mean as much as birth, but still an age when manners often meant more than morality.

Now Signet has commissioned some of its finest authors to write some bigger romances—longer, lusher, more exquisitely sensuous than ever before—wonderful love stories that encompass even more of the flavor of this glittering and flamboyant age. We are calling them "Super Regencies" because they have been liberated from category conventions and have the room to take the Regency novel even further—to the limits of the Regency itself.

Because we want to bring you only the very best, we are publishing these books only on an occasional basis, only when we feel that we can bring you something special. The first of the Super Regencies, *Love in Disguise* by Edith Layton, was published in August to rave reviews and has won two awards. It was followed by two other outstanding titles, *The Guarded Heart* by Barbara Hazard, published in October and *Indigo Moon* by Patricia Rice, published in February. Watch for future Signet Super Regencies in upcoming months in your favorite bookstore.

Sincerely,

Hilary Ross
Associate Executive Editor

A Difficult Truce

by
Joan Wolf

A SIGNET BOOK
NEW AMERICAN LIBRARY

NAL BOOKS ARE AVAILABLE AT QUANTITY DISCOUNTS
WHEN USED TO PROMOTE PRODUCTS OR SERVICES. FOR
INFORMATION PLEASE WRITE TO PREMIUM MARKETING
DIVISION, NEW AMERICAN LIBRARY, 1633
BROADWAY, NEW YORK, NEW YORK 10019.

Acknowledgments

Excerpts from the following poems are reprinted by permission:

"Under Ben Bulben," "Beautiful Lofty Things" and "The Statues": Reprinted with permission of Macmillan Publishing Co., Inc. from COLLECTED POEMS by William Butler Yeats. Copyright 1940 by Georgie Yeats, renewed in 1968 by Bertha Georgie Yeats, Michael Butler Yeats and Anne Yeats.

"Crazy Jane on the Day of Judgement." "I Am of Ireland" and "Remorse for Intemperate Speech": Reprinted with permission of Macmillan Publishing Co., Inc. from COLLECTED POEMS by William Butler Yeats. Copyright 1933 by Macmillan Publishing Co., Inc., renewed 1961 by Bertha Georgie Yeats.

"Meditations in Time of Civil War" and "Nineteen Hundred and Nineteen": Reprinted with permission of Macmillan Publishing Co., Inc. from COLLECTED POEMS by William Butler Yeats. Copyright 1921 by Macmillan Publishing Co., Inc., renewed 1956 by Georgie Yeats.

(The following page constitutes an extension of this copyright page.)

SIGNET TRADEMARK REG. U.S. PAT. OFF. AND FOREIGN COUNTRIES
REGISTERED TRADEMARK—MARCA REGISTRADA
HECHO EN CHICAGO, U.S.A.

SIGNET, SIGNET CLASSIC, MENTOR, ONYX, PLUME, MERIDIAN AND NAL BOOKS are published by NAL PENGUIN INC., 1633 Broadway, New York, New York 10019

FIRST SIGNET PRINTING, AUGUST, 1981

4 5 6 7 8 9 10 11 12

PRINTED IN THE UNITED STATES OF AMERICA

Author's Note

In this novel I have taken the liberty of compressing a whole century of Irish history into a few years' time. The battle for Catholic Emancipation was conducted in much the same fashion as I have described, only its leader was, of course, the great Daniel O'Connell. O'Connell ran as a candidate for Parliament in County Clare in 1828, and was elected. He could not take his seat, however, because, as a Catholic, he refused to take the preliminary oath. It was his election that forced the government to pass the Catholic Emancipation Bill in 1829.

Dacre's plan for making the Irish Party a force to be reckoned with in Parliament parallels the action taken later in the century when Charles Stewart Parnell headed the Irish Home Rule Party. It was Parnell's policy to win concessions for Ireland by impeding the conduct of regular parliamentary business in Westminster.

I have fictionalized the work and the personalities of O'Connell and Parnell and spread them among three imaginary characters: Christina MacCarthy, Dacre, and Murdoch Lynch. I hope those who love Irish history will not be offended and will realize my purpose was solely to create what I hope is a good story.

—Joan Wolf

Prologue

The news was brought to Lord Camden, Lord Lieutenant of Ireland. "The Earl of Clancarthy is dead." Lord Camden's expression revealed his satisfaction. "Splendid. I'll get a message off to London at once."

But for the great majority of the Irish people, the news was tragic. "Niall MacCarthy is dead," they said to each other, their faces lined with grief. And in the west, where for centuries the MacCarthy clan had ruled as princes, the word was even more devastating. MacCarthy More, MacCarthy the chief, the prince, the incomparable leader, MacCarthy More was dead.

The remaining leaders of the Executive Directory of United Irishmen met in emergency session. For them the news was nothing short of catastrophic.

Oliver Bond spoke first, his face gray and drained

in the fading winter light. "How did it happen?" he asked the room at large.

"He was betrayed, of course." Thomas Emmet spoke tiredly. "Someone gave the Castle information about his hiding place. He had a gun and killed five of them; but he was dead before they reached him."

They sat in the dim room, quiet in their grief, quiet in their desperation. Dr. William MacNevan spoke the words they were all thinking. "What are we going to do now?" They looked at him. "He was our one great hope, the last survivor of the great chiefs of old. Catholic Ireland would have risen to follow Niall Mac-Carthy. We would have been a nation once again." He bowed his head and repeated hopelessly, "What are we going to do?"

Bond looked at the faces gathered around the table. They had planned and schemed for so long. He thought of the floggings, the burnings, the murders that had been rampant since Parliament had instituted the Insurrection Act. He straightened in his chair. "We have no choice, gentlemen. The rising was scheduled for May and it must go forward. Besides," he peered around shrewdly, "all may not be lost. Clancarthy had a daughter."

"Yes," MacNevan spoke slowly, "we must rely on Christina now."

Charles Standish, Duke of Dacre and Home Secretary of His Majesty's government heard the news of Clancarthy's death with mingled relief and regret. "He was an extraordinary man," he said to William Pitt, the Prime Minister of Great Britain and the man who had just given him the news, "and the greatest threat to English rule in Ireland since Hugh O'Neill."

"Well, he is dead," Pitt replied flatly. "And Murdoch Lynch, his closest follower, is safe in Kilmainham

Gaol. Let us hope that any chance of rebellion in Ireland is quenched as well."

Dacre leaned back in his chair, one eyebrow raised skeptically. "What about Clancarthy's daughter?"

Silently, Pitt handed a document to Dacre, who scanned it with cool green eyes:

February 21, 1798
Dublin Castle

The Lord Lieutenant and Privy Council of Ireland have issued a proclamation declaring that they have received information upon oath, that *Lady Christina MacCarthy* has been guilty of High Treason, and offer a reward of 1,000 pounds sterling to any person who shall discover, apprehend, or commit her to prison.

Slowly, Dacre nodded. "Ordinarily I shouldn't think a woman dangerous in a situation like this, but Lady Christina is different. She was in France with her father last year and participated in his negotiations with the French Directory. I understand she made a very strong impression in Paris. And her mother was a German Royal Princess; her grandfather is King Ludwig of Letzau." He handed the paper back to the Prime Minister. "No, we cannot afford to ignore Lady Christina MacCarthy. I want her alive, though," and here Dacre rose to his great height and stared down his arrogant nose at Pitt. "Conferring martyrdom on the entire MacCarthy clan is not the way to, as you put it, 'quench rebellion' in Ireland."

"I realize that, Your Grace." Tiredly, Pitt rubbed his aching forehead. "Perhaps you will be good enough to speak to Lord Cornwallis before he leaves for Ireland to take up his new appointment as Lord Lieutenant."

Dacre's deep, clipped voice was even more decided than usual. "I should be happy to, Mr. Pitt," he said.

Lady Christina MacCarthy was at the MacCarthy residence outside of Killarney in County Kerry when a messenger arrived with the news of her father's death. All color drained from her face, but she took note of the man's obvious exhaustion and, with the unflagging courtesy she had learned from her parents, insisted on seeing him provided with food and drink. Then she left the house and headed her horse south, toward the height of Mangerton Mountain and the lovely, tranquil beauty of Muckross Abbey.

The February day was cold and sunny, the many groves and dells of Killarney clear in the harsh winter light. She stood for a moment on the shore of Lough Leane watching the shadows made by the circling birds on the shining lakewater, then she moved slowly toward the ruined Abbey. It had been built for the Franciscan friars in the fifteenth century by her ancestor, Donal MacCarthy Môr, and Christina had always found it a place of comfort and of peace. She went first to the ruined chancel, where so many chiefs of the MacCarthy clan lay buried. Then she went into the cloister.

This was the heart of the building and had mercifully escaped destruction at the hands of Cromwell's soldiers. Christina sat on the sill of one of the twenty-two graceful arches that made up the cloister and gazed at the magnificent yew tree which almost completely filled its center. Her father's voice seemed to float in the still and peaceful air:

"We cannot get the necessary legislative reforms, Christina. Wolfe Tone and I have done everything we can. They will allow Catholic forty-shilling freeholders

4

to vote, but they will not allow Catholics to sit in Parliament.

"The United Irishmen stand for two things, my darling, and finally, I stand for them too: a republican government and separation from England."

And, ultimately, "It will have to be a Rising, Christina. There can be no other way."

The echoes died away. Her mind felt leaden. She went back to the chancel and looked again at the tombs of her ancestors. "I am the chief now," she thought. But no emotion stirred; she felt frozen.

She walked down to the water's edge and stepped into the small boat she kept moored there. She rowed out into the beauty of Lough Leane, rested her oars, and let the boat float. All around her was the magnificence of Killarney: the jeweled water scattered with tiny islands made up of ravines and wooded cliffs; the circling mountains, guardians of the ancient kingdom of Kerry, dyed with blue and silver and rose. Her eyes moved from the water to the mountains to the sky. She thought, "He'll never see this again." And bowed her head and wept into the shining lakewater.

Chapter One

Then you should know that all things change in
   the world,
And hatred turns to love and love to hate....
                              —William Butler Yeats

William Pitt, Prime Minister of Great Britain, sat in
the government office at Westminster awaiting the
arrival of the Duke of Dacre. The King had just presented his Prime Minister with a problem of some
significance, and Pitt was about to pass it along to his
Home Secretary. He seemed to be doing that more
and more frequently these days.

Dacre was something of a puzzle to Pitt, as he was
to most of his colleagues in Parliament. He was a Standish, one of the foremost of the two hundred great
families who had been governing England for centuries. He was one of the wealthiest men in the king-

dom, owning some 186,000 acres in eleven counties. His ancestors had served in government since the fourteenth century, and when his father had died five years ago it had been expected by his family and his country that Charles would take his seat in Parliament and devote his prestige and talents to the governing of his country.

This he had done with notable success. In him, all the gifts of privilege had combined. He had wealth, blue blood, good looks, great charm, and, Pitt thought now, the finest brain he had known.

It was Dacre's impressive scholarship that tended to intimidate his peers. He was always impeccably courteous, but his courtesy failed to mask an underlying boredom with much of the business of government. While up at Trinity College, Cambridge, Dacre had taken a First in mathematics, but his abiding interest was geography. He still wrote scholarly articles for geographical journals, and Pitt had a deep suspicion that if Dacre were not held by the twin fetters of duty and heritage, he would be happily traveling in the Antipodes somewhere, making maps.

Pitt looked up now as Dacre entered the office. He watched the Duke carefully as he moved with the strong, fluid grace so unusual in so big a man to the one chair in the office he considered comfortable. It was a remarkable face, Pitt thought, with its sea-green eyes, hawk nose, and arrogant mouth. It was like a bronze mask cast by an ancient Greek, but what banked fires lay behind it remained Dacre's secret.

The Prime Minister laced his hands together on the desk in front of him and opened the subject that was most urgently on his mind.

"I have just come from the King. He is concerned about Lady Christina MacCarthy."

7

Dacre's eyes glinted under his shielding lashes. "I see. What does he want?"

"King Ludwig, His Majesty's dear cousin, is deeply worried about his beloved granddaughter. And His Majesty wishes to oblige King Ludwig. In short, he wants Lady Christina captured and released to the custody of her grandfather. And, Your Grace, you know how His Majesty is when he gets an idea into his head. Under the circumstances, I think it is best to placate him."

The mental instability of George the Third was a trial to his ministers. Dacre nodded agreement, but a thoughtful frown drew a faint line between his brows as he considered what Pitt had just told him. "The situation in Ireland is extremely tense, Mr. Pitt. We are in the midst of negotiating the union of Great Britain and Ireland, a measure we are both agreed is essential to bringing any kind of permanent order to Ireland. I don't want to jeopardize that."

"I understand the negotiations are going well."

A look of severe irony crossed Dacre's face. "The 'negotiations' consist of our buying out the votes of the Irish Parliament. They must agree to the union of our two Parliaments into one, which means they must literally vote themselves out of existence. Their agreeableness is costing us a great deal of money."

Pitt shrugged. "It has to be done, or we will have Ireland in a permanent state of rebellion."

"I know. Fortunately, the last one was put down relatively quickly. Except, of course, for Lady Christina. She has been holding out in the mountains of Kerry for over a year now. The Irish militia wouldn't touch her, you know. I had to get some of the Orange troops from Ulster and reinforce them with an English regiment."

"What precisely is the present situation, Your Grace?"

Dacre looked grim. "Difficult. I heard from Lord Cornwallis earlier this morning. Cope chased her out of the mountains, finally. She and about four hundred men are barricaded into the MacCarthy stronghold of Slea Castle. According to Cornwallis, it has walls fifteen feet thick and stands on a cliff overlooking the Atlantic. The rebels could hold off a force ten times their size. And there is no way to get cannon in over those mountains. We'll have to starve them out."

"How long, do you think, before they surrender?"

"Never. Cornwallis says they'll die first. He is extremely worried about the temper of the country. If we make a martyr out of Christina MacCarthy, we may have another Rising on our hands."

Pitt was alarmed. "I should say the situation is more than difficult, Your Grace. There is still the distinct possibility of a French invasion of Ireland. Not only that, we have been uncovering numerous plots among the Irish seamen in the Royal Navy."

"I know. The last conspiracy was to seize a man of war in the name of the United Irishmen, run up a green flag, and sail for France. I fear that their next plan will be to relieve Lady Christina."

"Don't be witty, Dacre," Pitt said sharply, real concern in his voice. "What do you suggest we do?"

"Rescue Lady Christina and send her home to grandpapa, I suppose." Dacre rose, his bright, fair hair suddenly burnished by a shaft of sunlight from the window. "Aside from placating the King, we really cannot afford to have the Union negotiations disturbed."

"I agree with your goals, Your Grace," Pitt said tartly. "Just how do you plan to accomplish them?"

"Oh, I shall think of something, Mr. Pitt," Dacre said, a trifle maliciously. "I'll leave for Ireland tomorrow."

Pitt relaxed as Dacre left the room. The Duke puzzled him and often irritated him, but he had implicit

9

trust in Dacre's abilities. He would resolve the matter of Lady Christina MacCarthy.

Had William Pitt known what the consequences of Dacre's mission would be, he would have recalled the Duke and forbidden him, on pain of death, to ever set foot in the Kingdom of Ireland.

Dacre spent that evening with his mistress of four years, Lady Maria Rochdale. His arrangement with Lady Maria suited him very well. She was beautiful, intelligent, discreet, and he saw her when he wanted to. Dacre had never yet met a woman he could bear the thought of actually living with. He doubted he ever would. His parents' marriage had been the model of an aristocratic alliance, but hardly one to induce admiration in their son. His father's passion was government, his mother's was society. Husband and wife met on occasion when their paths crossed at the same function. Neither had much interest in their only son, who was raised by tutors, grooms, and housekeepers. At twenty-five he had succeeded to the title. At twenty-eight, he was Home Secretary. He was not thirty years of age, unmarried, and—despite the lamentations of his aunts—likely to remain so.

They were at dinner in Lady Maria's house in fashionable Mount Street. The Duke, elegant himself in a well-cut black coat and snowy white shirt and waist coat, looked appreciatively across the candlelit table at his companion. Lady Maria's skin looked luminous in the candlelight, her black hair soft and shining.

And, at the moment, her sensuous mouth looked sulky. "Do you mean to say you have to go to Ireland just because of this rebel? Why can't the local troops handle it? She's only a woman."

Dacre smiled lazily. "Barely a woman," he said. "She isn't twenty yet. But, my pet, she is trouble. The King wants her safe, and unless I come up with a brilliant stroke, she is going to end up very dead."

Lady Maria shook her head. "I still don't understand how a girl like that could be so dangerous."

"She is dangerous, Maria, not because she is a woman, but because she is a MacCarthy."

"I never heard of the MacCarthys."

He smiled at her tone, but answered seriously, "The MacCarthys are one of the only great native Irish families left. They have money; they own half of Kerry and made a fortune smuggling wool to France. They are Catholic."

Lady Maria looked puzzled. "I thought the penal laws forbade Catholics to own land in Ireland."

"They did. The Earl of Sherbourne is a Protestant neighbor of the MacCarthys. From 1704 to 1782 the Sherbournes held the MacCarthy lands in their name. In '82 they were ceded back to Niall MacCarthy, Christina's father. The problem," Dacre's brows were furrowed now, "the problem is that for centuries Kerry has lain virtually beyond the normal administration of the law. The Earl of Clancarthy was king in all but name. And the peasants are fiercely loyal to their last remaining chief. Who now happens to be a nineteen-year-old girl."

"I see," she smiled at him, her blue eyes darkening. "Well, I only hope you won't be gone for too long, Charles. I want you at my ball in May."

He laughed. "Your priorities, my pet, are impeccable as always." His own eyes narrowed. "But, Maria, I had plans for this evening other than talking about Christina MacCarthy."

She rose from the table. "By all means, Your Grace," she said demurely, and led the way upstairs.

When Dacre landed in Ireland, he went immediately to Dublin Castle to meet with the Lord Lieutenant. Cornwallis was delighted to see him. "Things are progressing well with the Union, Your Grace. Lord Castlereagh has been diligent in using the full weight of the Castle to persuade members of the Irish Parliament to vote in favor of uniting the Kingdom of Ireland to the Kingdom of Great Britain."

"How diligent, my lord?"

"Well, we haven't exactly been handing out money, but where individuals might be influenced by rewards of title or of office to support the Union, we have been generous."

"How generous?"

Cornwallis grimaced. "Sixteen borough owners have been given English peerages, twenty-eight Irish peerages have been created, and twenty Irish peerages have been increased in rank."

Dacre looked stunned. "My God, you have been busy."

"It is a dirty business, Your Grace, I grant you that. But if we want the Union, the Irish Parliament must vote for it. And it is not easy to get people to vote their own legislature out of existence."

"I suppose not. There'll be a fuss about the scale of these, ah, rewards."

Cornwallis looked stubborn. "If there are no rewards, there will be no Union. And, Your Grace, without the Union the British Empire must be dissolved."

Dacre was unimpressed by Cornwallis's rhetoric, but knew that essentially he was correct. "Well, I'll support you with Pitt, my lord. But what I really came over here to discuss was the problem of Lady Christina MacCarthy."

Cornwallis looked gloomy. "The situation remains the same, Your Grace. The rebels are still inside Slea Castle, with our troops camped outside. They won't surrender. Already, there has been unrest in the country. She was less trouble when she was at large than she is likely to prove at present. Bonfires have been lit in vigil all around the countryside. If we starve Christina MacCarthy to death in Slea Castle, we may be faced with a Catholic rising we won't be able to put down."

Dacre was unperturbed. "The King doesn't want her dead. She is the granddaughter of King Ludwig of Letzau, a distant cousin of the House of Hanover. Our orders are to be sure no royal blood is spilt."

Cornwallis rose to his feet and paced around the room. He came back to stand in front of the Duke, who regarded him calmly. "How, Your Grace, are we to manage that? She is just not going to surrender. She's like her father. She'd rather die."

"I realize that, my lord. I think I have a solution that will avoid bloodshed on all sides."

Cornwallis was blunt. "How?"

Dacre told him.

"It's risky," the Lord Lieutenant said thoughtfully when he had finished. "With the state the country is in, I confess I don't know what to do."

"We haven't much choice," Dacre said evenly. "The King wants her alive; you want her alive. Our options, under the circumstances, are somewhat limited."

Cornwallis rubbed his forehead. "You are right, unfortunately. I hope it works, Your Grace. I have one suggestion, however."

"Yes?"

"If you succeed, you still have to get her to Dublin. Take an escort of English troops with you. I wouldn't trust the Irish." He poured a glass of wine for the Duke.

Dacre nodded and accepted the glass. "The King will hardly want her thrown into the common jail, since he's taken so much trouble over saving her neck. Where shall I bring her?"

Cornwallis frowned. "I wouldn't want her in Kilmainham Gaol, anyway. I don't think it's secure enough. Bring her here to the Castle. The Bermingham Tower will hold her well enough."

Dacre put down his glass and rose. "Will you assign me an escort?" At Cornwallis's nod, he made for the door. "I'll leave tomorrow at seven. Good afternoon, my lord."

As Dacre rode across Ireland toward Kerry, he found himself shocked by the poverty he saw around him. The people were a ragged, starving lot, their homes fit only for demolition. Accustomed to the well-fed, well-scrubbed look of his own tenants, he was horrified by the skinny, hungry children he saw around him on all sides.

The word had gone out, as it always did in Ireland, as to who he was. He was met in every town with silent, hostile crowds of people, who gazed upon his retinue with sullen hatred. For the first time he began to appreciate what Cornwallis had been talking about when he had spoken of the country as a powder keg.

As he passed out of Tipperary, with its rich valley land and green glens, and headed toward Kerry, the scenery began to change. The lovely, lonely countryside, with its mountains and lakes, reminded him somewhat of his own home country of Cumberland in the north of England. Here too in MacCarthy country he noticed the improved lot of the peasantry. Farms were well-kept, and people decently dressed and shod. The crowds that stared at him were made up of women, children, and old men. The young men and the boys, he thought, with a wry twist of the mouth, were probably all in Slea Castle with Lady Christina.

He left Tralee and crossed the Conor Pass onto the Dingle Peninsula. The Slieve Mish mountains rose all around him, dotted with small lakes. Dacre had the feeling that he was moving back in time, entering a

14

world foreign to his modern cynicism and sensibility. This feeling increased drastically as he approached the savage promontory of land called Slea Head. It was a flat, eerie expanse of rock, swept by Atlantic gales and half ringed with wild mountains. All over Slea Head were prehistoric beehive-like dwellings of stone. They were scattered in countless numbers, singly and in groups. It was in this vast deserted city set on the tractless, stony waste of Slea Head that Dacre found the British army.

Colonel Cope came to meet him, and registered deep surprise when he realized who Dacre was. "The rebels are this way, Your Grace," he said. Dacre moved with him to a cluster of clochans, as the stone huts were called, and saw Slea Castle. It stood, impregnable, poised five hundred feet above the sea on the edge of a sheer wall of dark, foam-lashed rock. Its walls were of thick gray stone. It had one large gate for entrance and small slits in the rock for marksmen. It would be a slaughter to try to storm it.

"We've already had five men killed, Your Grace," Colonel Cope reported to Dacre. "They strayed within range of the guns. We're going to have to starve them out."

Dacre's eyes were focused on the grim stone walls. "I don't think so." He looked at Cope. "Can we get a message to them?"

"They'll respect a white flag, I think." Cope was blunt. "Why, Your Grace?"

"I have a proposal to make to Lady Christina."

"And what may that be, Your Grace?"

"I propose to offer pardons to the entire rebel force, if Lady Christina will surrender herself to me. I will then convey her, under escort, to Dublin."

Dark color flooded Cope's face. "Let them go?" he said incredulously. "You can't mean it!"

"But I do," the Duke said smoothly. He unbent so

far to explain. "This is not a military situation, Colonel Cope, it is a political one. The King does not want Lady Christina harmed. Can you guarantee her safety if you 'starve them out'?"

"Of course not!"

"Can you think of any other terms on which she might surrender?"

The answer was grudging. "No."

"This is the only way. The rebellion is over, and they know it. Without Lady Christina, the rest of them will be harmless. But we must secure her."

Cope looked at the man standing opposite. There was authority in every line of his face, every clipped tone of his voice. The Colonel nodded. "I'll find someone to deliver your message, Your Grace."

Twenty minutes later they stood watching as a veteran English sergeant moved on horseback across the ground between camp and castle. As he reached the walls of Slea, he was met by a rebel. They spoke briefly in front of the great gate; then the Englishman, having handed over his letter, turned his horse and headed back toward the camp.

Christina MacCarthy stood in the middle of the great hall of Slea Castle, looking at the sheet of paper in her hand. Men were spread around the vast space in small groups; some were playing cards, others talking in low voices. All eyes, surreptitiously, were fixed on her. Her eyes were focused on the signature, Charles Standish, Duke of Dacre, but she did not see it. Her mind was elsewhere, turned in upon herself, to the secret well of strength and belief where she made her decisions.

What choice had she? If it was only her own life that was at issue, there would be a choice. But the decision she made would affect other lives as well. While there was a chance of success, she would lead men into danger. But when all was lost, how could she wantonly throw away other lives? While she had had no other way out, she had been prepared to put her back to the wall and hold on—to the death if necessary. Better that than surrender to a hangman's rope. But now, they could all go free. Except her.

Dacre's signature came into focus before her eyes. Could she trust him? She looked around and the seventeen-year-old face of young Liam Emmet met her eyes. A tremor crossed her own face. She would have to trust him. Calling for pen and paper, she sat down to write an answer. Her men wouldn't like it. But they would obey her. They always did.

Christina's answer arrived by messenger at the English camp at precisely eight o'clock that night. Dacre raised his green eyes from the missive and looked at Colonel Cope. "She has agreed. She wants her men to be allowed to leave first. After they are safely gone, she will surrender."

Cope frowned. "I don't like it."

Dacre's voice was short. "She doesn't trust us. Why should she? Do you have any men who know what she looks like?"

"Yes."

"Good. We'll set up a check point for her men to pass through. We don't want her slipping through our fingers again."

"No, by God!" Cope was fervent.

The exodus started at nine the next morning. The Irish were obviously unhappy. They looked back frequently at the unyielding walls of Slea Castle. Dacre was impressed by the authority Lady Christina had exerted to bend them to her decision. It took two hours to check them all through.

The April winds were driving wild, dappled clouds across the sky when a lone figure appeared in the great door of Slea Castle's outer wall. Slowly a gray horse

17

moved across the treeless expanse of rock toward the English camp. Dacre, mounted on a shining black, went to meet her.

He had never wondered what she looked like. But he knew, as their horses moved closer together, he hadn't expected this. Her horse stopped five feet in front of his. "Christ!" he thought.

Eyes gray as the rain-washed Atlantic looked into his from under straight brows. Her hair, pale as moonlight, was loosely pulled off her face and fell in a single braid between her shoulders. Her brow was wide and grave; her skin glowed gold from the sun. He felt his breathing alter. He had never seen a face of such flawless beauty.

"I am Christina MacCarthy." Her voice was cold and pure, the voice of a choirboy. "I am here to surrender myself to the Duke of Dacre."

"I am Dacre." He was relieved his voice sounded normal. "In the name of His Majesty, King George the Third, I take you prisoner. My duty is to escort you to Dublin, where you will be delivered up to the Lord Lieutenant for imprisonment on the charge of high treason."

Not a muscle in her face moved. The gray eyes took in the troops camped behind him. "Do you need an army to escort me, Duke?"

"Not if you will give me your word not to try to escape."

Her eyes flickered at that and she made a gesture indescribably weary. "The game is over, Duke. I know that. I give you my word."

They left with an escort of twenty English soldiers two hours later.

Chapter Two

A girl arose that had red mournful lips
And seemed the greatness of the world in tears,
Doomed like Odysseus and the labouring ships
And proud as Priam murdered with his peers....
—William Butler Yeats

They left Slea Head and headed along the coast toward Dingle. The sky was filled with racing clouds, brightening or darkening the waters of the bay, alternately veiling and unveiling the mountains in the distance. The air smelled of salt. Dacre stole a glance at the girl riding so silently beside him. She had scarcely spoken two words since they started. They rode in careful formation, armed horsemen before and behind her, Dacre at her side. He was taking no chances. She had given him her word not to try to escape, but that didn't necessarily preclude an attempt to rescue her. He looked once more at her profile, then at her hands on

19

the reins. They were capable hands, firm and strong, except for the wrists which were delicately boned and fragile. What was she thinking?

Christina had retreated deep within herself. As the horses had moved off and the Duke, so formidably big, had fallen in beside her, panic had struck. For the first time she realized as fact what had happened. She was going to prison. And then to her death. Awash in terror, she deliberately withdrew her attention from her surroundings and concentrated on the stampeding flood inside. This was not the first time she had faced her own fear. The decision to take arms against England; the first time she was in battle; the first time she had killed a man: she knew fear and she knew by now how to deal with it. So she let it flood through her until it seemed there was nothing else in the world but the hammering of her heart and the heaving of her stomach and then, suddenly, it was gone, the flood receding as quickly as it had come.

So, on the first few hours of that long journey across Ireland, Christina MacCarthy faced her fear of her own death, and won the battle. Dacre, glancing so curiously at her set face, had no clue as to what it concealed.

They had been traveling for half a day when the phenomenon that was to dog their whole journey first occurred. They were coming down a narrow mountain road, passing off the Dingle Peninsula with its vast stony silence, when a line of old peasants mysteriously appeared, standing silently just off the road. As the Duke and Christina came abreast of them, they saw the tears that poured down the lined old faces. In a quavering voice one cried out to her in Irish; the others began to sob. Christina turned the grave beauty of her face toward them and spoke softly in the same language. Dacre found himself staring in surprise. It was *her* voice that was offering comfort.

When they had left the peasants behind, he turned to her. "What did they want?"

She shook her head. "Nothing. They were just distressed to find me under these circumstances." Her gray gaze flickered over the English soldiers who surrounded her.

"They called you 'MacCarthy More'?"

"It is the traditional name for the chief of the MacCarthy clan. It was used long before the English 'Earl of Clancarthy' was given. It is the last truly Irish title in Ireland," she said. "It will die with me."

Dacre said nothing.

As they traveled further, moving slowly because of the roads, it became clear that word of Christina's capture had gone before them. All along their route were massed the evidence of her power. Some stood silent and grief-stricken, others called out her name. Dacre heard again and again the words "MacCarthy More." He felt once again the eerie sensation of being in some other world; it was as if he were back in ancient time, escorting some great Celtic chieftain to a fiery doom. He kept his horse close to the slender girl riding so quietly beside him. Her composure and her compassion for them stunned him.

They made camp for the night in a secluded valley. The campfire was made in a small clearing surrounding by winter-bare thickets of rhododendron. Food was prepared.

One of the soldiers, a fleshy, ugly-looking man, came up to Christina with a bowl of stew. "Here you are, Your Ladyship." His voice was an insult, his eyes raked her figure. As he handed her her food he contrived to touch her fingers. Christina resisted the impulse to wipe her hand and watched him go, her eyes thoughtful.

It grew cooler as the sun went down and the men gathered around the fire, except for the guards posted in a circle behind them. Christina sat a little apart from the men, on a wide flat rock. She had put a rough brown wool cloak on over her heavy knit sweater. Dacre watched her, sitting so quietly, the firelight dim compared to her pure, shining beauty. He walked over to her and sat down, his back against his saddle and blanket.

"The Irish love a martyr," he remarked, a hint of acid in his deep voice. "Unfortunately for you, they are more inclined to make one than they are to prevent the martyrdom's occurring in the first place."

Christina turned to him, her gray eyes darkening with dawning anger. "What are you talking about?" she said shortly.

For some reason he did not understand, he was angry himself, but the cool, level tone of his voice remained the same. "I mean that it is easy to weep, less easy to act." He looked at her slender, tense figure and clear, fine-boned face. "Tell me, Lady Christina, did you expect the rebellion to be successful?"

"It had a chance," she said briefly.

"It had a very good chance," he said. "You had us scared to death." He looked at his own hands, long and elegant, clasped now around the knees of his buckskin breeches. "Why didn't they follow you, Lady Christina?"

She looked at him consideringly. The firelight cast shadows on his face and drew gold sparks from his hair. He had sounded genuinely interested. Why not try to make him understand, she thought. She had nothing to lose and Ireland perhaps would gain.

"We had a great cause," she began, "Wolfe Tone and my father and the rest of the United Irishmen. We wanted to throw you out and give Ireland back to the people who once owned her before the conquerors came with their alien garrison of landlords and clergy. It was to be a political revolution, like the one that

22

happened in America." She gestured with her hand, a movement indescribably lovely, and her voice sounded weary. "But what do politics mean to the ignorant, ill-used, and hungry masses of the Irish people? Nothing. They know only the landlord."

She paused, then said more urgently, "Do you know, Your Grace, what the land system is in Ireland?" Her eyes searched his shadowed face.

"I know it was a cause of deep dissatisfaction, but I confess I was not prepared for the poverty I have seen among the peasants here."

She sat silent for a moment, gathering her thoughts. When she spoke her voice was resolutely dispassionate, clear and precise as a teacher's lecturing on a matter of historical research. "Ninety percent of the Irish people live off the land," she began. "There is, quite literally, no other means of existence, Irish manufacture having been most successfully discouraged by the English government. The land is owned by a small number of aristocrats, mostly Protestant. It is leased out to the peasants. In most cases, however, the peasant does not lease it from the owner, but from someone who has bought the right to lease it out. In some cases there are as many as seven people between the man working the land and the owner of that land. And they all want their profit."

"There is wholesale leasing of farms in England, too," he said, "but the result is not the poverty I see here."

"The Irish peasant, unlike the English, has no security of tenure in the land he leases, Your Grace. He can be thrown off his farm at the whim of the landlord, and often is. The landlord's policy is to rack the tenant for the highest rent possible, and if he can't pay, he has to go. The farms are in such wretched condition because the tenant must first of all pay for any improvements himself and then he finds the rent has been raised because the property is now 'more desirable.'

"The masses of the Irish people, my lord Duke, raise livestock for the landlord and subsist themselves on potatoes. If they are turned off their land, there is no other way for them to live. They starve to death, Your Grace."

"And if the potatoes fail?"

"Then they starve also. There was a blight in the west three years ago. My father imported wheat from America and personally fed all his tenants and as many more as he could. But many died. And they died while their landlords were exporting food to England."

She was sitting poised on the edge of her rock, her face bright with intensity. "The ownership of property has responsibilities, Duke, as well as privileges. But the Irish Parliament recognizes only the privileges. One of the reasons for this," her clear voice was deeply bitter, "is that Protestants own most of the land. And only Protestants may sit in Parliament."

The moon went behind a cloud. His face was mysteriously shadowed, but his voice, deep and even, was clear. "Then it is land reform you want, not necessarily independence."

"We thought independence was the best way to achieve land reform, but if another way could be found, I would take it." From under level brows her eyes met and held his steadily. "You were scornful because the people did not rise and fight. Sometimes those who have almost nothing find it hardest to let go what little they do have. They know, you see, what utter devastation is. The Irish peasant, Your Grace, is born with a stone in his fist. If my death would help them, I'd go to it gladly. It is my grief that I have failed. My death will do them no good."

He sat silent, shaken by her sincerity and by her misconception. He was not taking Christina Mac-

Carthy to her death. But some instinct kept him from telling her of the government's plans to release her to her grandfather. There was a quality of dedication about this girl that both moved and frightened him. He was relieved when the voice of Captain Harris demanded his attention.

She saw him rise and stood also. Tall herself, she was surprised again at how far she had to look up to see his face. His shoulders were so wide they blocked the entire scene behind him. His voice, when it came, startled her by its harshness. "We must talk of this again, Lady Christina. But now, good night." And he moved off toward the rest of the men.

Christina arranged her blanket competently on the hard ground. She was used to living rough, used to protecting her privacy, the only woman in a large body of men. She washed her face and hands with water from her canteen, brushed out her hair and re-braided it, then lay down. Curled on her side with her eyes closed, she murmured her prayers and fell asleep.

"Lady Christina!" The whispered words brought her awake. She sat up and glanced swiftly around her. The Duke lay some twelve feet from her wrapped in his blanket, asleep. The rest of the camp was sleeping as well, except for the guards posted in a circle behind them.

Silent as the mist, Liam Emmet had slipped past the guard and knelt now beside her, calling her name. "Lady Christina!" He stopped when he saw her sit up.

"Liam!" Her voice was barely a thread. "What are you doing here?"

"I've come to rescue you." His voice rose a bit in his excitement. "Padraic and five others are waiting beyond, with horses. We have only to slip by the guard and we'll away from this place."

She was silent a moment, then said, "I can't go with

25

you, Liam. I gave my word of honor to the Duke not to try to escape."

"Ahh." His tone gave clear evidence of his feelings. "What can a word to an Englishman signify? Did any one of them ever keep their word to us?"

Her voice was crisper. "That's not the point, Liam. Besides, what would I do if I escaped with you? Fight again?" At his suddenly flaming face, she shook her head. "It's no good, Liam. We tried it, and we failed. It's all over with."

His voice betrayed his incredulity. "It's not over! All over Ireland people are talking of nothing but you. If you escape, they'll rally to you by the thousands."

But she was still shaking her head. "No, they won't, Liam. And even if they did, it would still be of no use." Her voice was sober and clear, perfectly audible to Dacre who, contrary to appearances, was not asleep. "We have no arms, Liam, and what's more to the point, we have no trained leaders. Napoleon Bonaparte is running France now; he has no interest in Ireland. Our chances of success always depended on French aid, but that won't be coming now." Her eyes, wide pools of gray in the moonlight, looked with compassion at the anxious brown eyes watching her. "I will not fight, Liam. I will not have any more deaths on my conscience." He began to speak and she cut him off. "Nor will I flee the country. I would rather die than turn my back on Ireland."

Tears rained down his young face, his voice was choked. "I can't leave you with them. They'll kill you."

Her voice was gentle but final. "You have no choice, Liam. I won't say that I'm not afraid, because I am. But I have the strangest feeling that what I do now will be of great importance to us all." She shrugged and laughed a little. "I don't know how, I just feel it."

"How can your death benefit us?" He was angry.

26

"I don't know. I only know I have to do what I think is right."

He looked at her adamant face and knew she meant what she said. His heart was torn, but for over a year he had given her absolute obedience. It was a habit not easily broken. "God be with you, MacCarthy More," he whispered in Irish.

"And with you, Liam Emmet," she answered in the same language.

He was gone, silent and unnoticed as he had learned to be during the last year and a half.

He was gone. For some minutes she remained sitting, her forehead pillowed on her knees. She had rejected her last chance at safety. The shadow of death seemed very close to her as she sat alone in the moonlight. She shivered. She had spoken the truth to Liam; she was afraid.

The Duke of Dacre lay awake long after she had fallen back to sleep. He was deeply stirred by the one thing that had always had the power to move him: courage. For all she knew she could have escaped. But she had chosen to sacrifice herself rather than bring more suffering on her country. It was not easy to choose death, when one was vital and lovely and nineteen years old.

He lay quiet, watching the sky as clouds moved in to cover the stars and the moon. Shortly before sunrise he heard her cry out, and half rose from his blanket. She sat up abruptly, her breath wheezing in her throat, and raised shaking hands to her neck as though she could still feel the hangman's rope choking her. Her eyes, black with fear, met his. Her mouth quivered and with a violent motion she turned her back on him and lay down again. Dacre looked at his own hands. They were shaking also.

Chapter Three

What could have made her peaceful with a mind
That nobleness made simple as a fire,
With beauty like a tightened bow, a kind
That is not natural in an age like this,
Being high and solitary and most stern?

— William Butler Yeats

The next day was cold and overcast. Neither Christina nor the Duke made any reference to the events of the night before. They had breakfast and were in the saddle by seven. They day grew steadily colder; the wind was sharp and chill. Dacre glanced uneasily at the sky, then to the profile of the girl who rode beside him. She was dressed warmly enough in breeches, sweater, and cloak, but it was going to rain and Dacre rode ahead to Captain Harris.

"Is there someplace we can get under cover, Captain?" he asked. "I don't relish the idea of riding all day in a rainstorm."

The soldier looked at the mountains stretching around them on all sides. "Not until we get out of the mountains, Your Grace. There is a garrison near Ballingarry; another couple of hours, I'd say."

Dacre nodded and dropped back. A half an hour later the rains came, cold, penetrating, unrelenting. The horses' hooves made soft, sucking sounds as the road slowly turned to mud. Dacre turned up the collar of his coat and saw Christina burrow into her own cloak. The rain soaked through the wool and dripped down their necks. It was two more hours before they reached the small fort outside of Ballingarry. As they rode into the courtyard, Dacre glanced at her with admiration. She had made not one complaint. But she looked frozen.

Speaking with all his formidable authority, Dacre made clear to the commander what he wanted. In five minutes, Christina found herself in the commander's bedroom, with a fire going strongly. She took off her wet cloak and sweater and crouched before the warmth of the fire. By the time Dacre returned her teeth had stopped chattering.

He carried a hot drink which he gave to her. She sipped it gratefully, then coughed. "What's in it?" she gasped.

He smiled. "One of the things Ireland does best. Whiskey. Drink it, it'll chase the cold out."

Very few people could resist Charles Standish's rare smile. It was young, mischievous, and utterly charming. Her mouth curved in reply and she took another cautious sip. He still had on his own wet coat and she raised an eyebrow at him. "Are you contemplating suicide by pneumonia, Duke? Why don't you get out of that coat?"

He put down his drink. "Good idea." He spread his

coat on a chair next to hers and dragged two more chairs to the fire. "Have a seat, Lady Christina. I don't think we'll be going anywhere for quite some time."

She sat down beside him and they both stretched their booted feet toward the fire. They sat in a silence that was oddly companionable, feeling the warmth of the whiskey inside and of the fire on their skin.

"I have been thinking of our discussion yesterday," he said. She turned and looked at him. His eyes were on the fire. His hair had begun to feather as it dried, coppery gold at the tips, and the firelight struck sparks of green from beneath his lowered lashes. He was still and his voice was quiet, but the power of his personality filled the room. Her own eyes were wide as she watched him, judging him as she had not done before.

He turned and met her gaze. "Do you know what is happening in Dublin?" he asked. "Do you know about the Union?"

"I have heard talk of it."

"The Prime Minister—and I—want to see the two countries of England and Ireland joined into a United Kingdom. To do this, the Irish Parliament must vote to dissolve itself and send instead representatives to the Parliament in London. You would have one hundred seats in the Commons and a decent representation in the Lords."

She spoke impatiently. "The Irish Parliament is the Parliament of the Protestant Ascendancy, Duke. It little matters to the country what happens to it."

He transferred his gaze from her face back to the fire. His voice was detached. "What if the Union also meant Catholic Emancipation? What if Catholics were allowed to sit at Westminster, Lady Christina? Would that be of little interest to you?"

She sat up straight on her chair and stared at him. "Is that going to happen?"

He said carefully, "We wanted to put through the
30

Union and full Catholic Emancipation together. Mr. Pitt was for it, I was for it, Lord Cornwallis was for it. But Lord Clare was not."

"And Lord Clare, the premier representative of the Protestant Ascendancy, has, as usual, won." Her voice was brittle. "My father wanted Catholic Emancipation, Your Grace. He fought for it. So did Wolfe Tone. If Parliament was reformed and the percentage of the country who are Catholic could elect their own, the necessary social changes could be done by legislation. But Lord Clare and his party are hardly going to allow that. They would lose all their privileges."

He spoke slowly. "I know. And we need Clare if we want to get the Union passed. But once it is accomplished, we are pledged to bring in Catholic Emancipation. Catholics may not have been able to sit in the Irish Parliament, but they will be able to sit at Westminster."

Christina's voice was scornful in reply. "In an Irish Parliament, my lord Duke, we would be the majority and thus able to make the legislation we need. At Westminster we would always be the minority, subject—as ever—to the will of the Protestant, land-owning, majority. Catholic Emancipation for an English parliament will hardly help Ireland."

"Why not give us a chance?" he said. "We are in the process of joining our people together in a political union of enormous consequence. Perhaps the people of England will be more sympathetic to the plight of Ireland than your own aristocratic landowners have been."

Her finely cut lips twisted for a moment, wryly, "I doubt it, Duke. But, then, I won't be around to see the outcome, I'm afraid."

There was a pause, then he said quietly, "What makes you so sure you will be executed?"

"Wolfe Tone was."

31

"Wolfe Tone was not a cousin of the King of England."

"What do you mean?"

"Why do you think I bargained for your surrender? You hadn't a chance; you know that. We didn't have to let your men go free. We could have starved you out."

Gray and fathomless, her eyes searched his. "What do you want of me?" Her voice was barely audible.

"Not your death. The King expressly ordered that your life was not to be endangered. I believe your grandfather has been insistent on your behalf."

Her eyes never wavered. "Not my death, only my freedom." At the look on his face she swung out of her chair and walked to the window. The rain still poured down. He looked at her silent back, and his mouth set into a grim line. The issue of Christina's future needed to be handled with the utmost care, and he judged he had given her enough to think about for the present. Quietly, he left the room. For a long time she stayed where she was, staring, unseeing, at the rain.

The weather cleared overnight and they started again early the next morning. Their route was once again lined with people, and the silent crowds, so obviously hostile to the English soldiers, caused Captain Harris distinct uneasiness. The soldiers rode in strict formation, guns to hand, surrounding the slender girl who was the cause of all the unrest.

Christina felt her senses were heightened during that ride. The air seemed clearer, the countryside more beautiful, the faces of her countrymen dearer. And always, she was conscious of the Duke of Dacre, ever at her side, organizing and directing everything that pertained to her.

The third night out they spent at the country house of the Earl of Clonmel, in Tipperary. The Earl and

Countess happened to be at home, and eagerly welcomed the English Duke. Christina was assigned a bedroom, with a soldier to guard her door, and the rest of her escort made camp in the park.

Christina used the opportunity to take a bath and wash her hair. It was blissful, after a year and a half of deprivation, to soak luxuriously in a hot tub and wash her hair in warm water. That she had the Duke to thank for her treat she had no doubt. Lord and Lady Clonmel would hardly have bestirred themselves on her behalf.

Dacre was dining with the Earl and Countess and had the opportunity to get a firsthand account of how the Irish Protestant nobility felt about Christina MacCarthy. The Clonmels were hospitable and gracious; they obviously felt that entertaining the Duke was a great honor. They just as obviously would have liked to see Christina dead.

"If we don't make an example of her, my lord Duke," said Lord Clonmel, "there's no telling what may happen."

"Surely she will be safe hundreds of miles away in Letzau, my lord," Dacre answered.

"Ah, but will she go?" Clonmel asked shrewdly. "I gather you will make her the same offer that was made to the other United Irish leaders: Freedom if she promises to exile herself forever from Ireland. Murdoch Lynch wouldn't promise, and he is still in prison in Dublin. Will Lady Christina agree to exile?"

Christina's words to young Liam Emmet two nights ago were in his mind. "I don't know," Dacre said slowly.

"I tell you frankly, Christina MacCarthy in jail in Dublin is dangerous." Lord Clonmel was intensely serious as he leaned across the table toward Dacre. "The peasants looked upon Clancarthy as an uncrowned

33

King. This girl is now the focal point of all national sentiment in the country."

"The papists see her as a sort of Virgin Mary, I believe," put in the Countess.

"I tell you, Duke, I don't care whose granddaughter she is," concluded Clonmel. "She is better dead."

Dacre went to see Christina before he retired that evening. He found her still dressed in her shabby clothes, with skin glowing from her bath. Her hair, almost dry, hung to her shoulders, a pale hood of silver. She smiled at him gratefully. "Thank you for your thoughtfulness. The bath was wonderful."

His face looked taut, but his voice was even. "Good. Is there anything else you need?"

She bit her lip, hesitated, then spoke in a low tone. "I wonder if you could see to it that one of the soldiers, his name is Dibden, is not assigned to guard me."

His eyes, searching her face, were very green. "Why?"

She gave a tiny shrug. "It's nothing, I suppose. I just don't like the way he looks at me."

His voice was very clipped. "I'll see to it." He moved to the door and turned to look at her once more. "The Clonmels want your blood," he said.

"Of course they do. They represent everything I was fighting against."

"I could see that." Suddenly he smiled. "Good night, Lady Christina. Sleep well." The door closed behind him, but Christina stood for a long time looking at its polished wood. The room seemed very empty without him.

They were in Kildare by the fourth day. The crowds had dwindled as they moved east; Kildare had been brutally crushed in the Rebellion and Christina's supporters feared to come out into the open. The troops relaxed their vigilance a trifle and Christina and the

Duke had a chance to talk as they rode across the vast plain of the Curragh.

"Have you ever met your grandfather?" Dacre asked her carefully. "He has expended a great deal of effort in your behalf, you know."

She smiled briefly. "Yes, twice. Once Mama took me, when I was ten. That was the year before she died. Then, when I went to France with Papa a few years ago we paid a visit to Letzau."

He knew what her visit to France had entailed, but chose to ignore it. "I've never been to Letzau."

"Not too many people have. It is a small country, and very well run. The roads are good, the peasants well fed and orderly, and health care is excellent. Grandpapa is a King who works at it. So did my mother when she lived there."

"Your mother was his only daughter?"

"Yes. Uncle Karl is his heir, but Mama was his favorite. He was not at all happy when she fell in love with my father. But she held out for three years and refused to marry anyone else. In the end he had to give in."

He said, seemingly irrelevantly, "Ireland is not like Letzau."

The edges of her mouth curled. "It certainly isn't, Duke. And I don't think Mama ever quite got used to it." Her voice softened. "But she was happy. She had my father."

"And you."

"A dubious pleasure for much of the time," she said briskly. "What delightful accommodation do you have planned for tonight?"

"The army barracks," he said calmly.

"I see," she said slowly, her eyes on the expressionless profile he turned toward her.

They reached the barracks about dusk and Christina looked with darkened eyes at the large fortification, symbol of the enemy's superior military power. The militia was not there at present, only a small garrison of English troops. A soldier, under Dacre's orders, brought her to one of the officer's quarters, then left her alone.

The room was spartan, but there was a bed, and to Christina sleeping in a bed was still a luxury of the highest order. The room was distinctly chilly, however, and there was no wood with which to start a fire. Christina went to the door and looked out. For once, there was no soldier on guard, nor was there anyone within sight. She closed the door and went to look out the back window. Piled only a few feet from the back of the building was a stack of wood.

Christina went swiftly to the door and stepped out. There was still no one in sight, so she shrugged slightly and started to walk around the long narrow building to get the wood for herself. She was not unnoticed.

Thomas Dibden had been keeping Christina under close observation since they left Slea Head. He had been able to get close to her only once or twice, but his eyes had rarely left her figure. Christina had been aware of his gaze, which is why she had asked Dacre to see he was kept away from her. She had lived with only men for over a year, but there was something in Dibden's eyes that made her very uneasy.

When Dibden had seen Christina's escort come back alone, he had slipped quietly away. He was hidden in the shadow of a doorway when he saw her come out and look around. He waited a few minutes and was beginning to move toward her lodging when she came out again and started to walk briskly around the building. He followed.

Dacre was deep in consultation with Captain Harris. "I suggest, Your Grace, that we bring Lady Christina into Dublin late at night," the soldier was saying.

"Dublin mobs can be very ugly and we don't want her hurt now we've got her this far."

"Dublin doesn't approve of Lady Christina, I take it."

"They'd be out with rocks and rotten fruit if they knew we were coming," the Captain said bluntly. "Those that support her, and there are a number of them, would be frightened into staying at home."

Dacre thought of Christina's proud, lovely face and spoke decisively. "I don't want to subject Lady Christina to any harrassment. When do you suggest we bring her in?"

"After midnight."

The Duke nodded. "All right. We'll begin at our usual time tomorrow and stop halfway to Dublin to rest. If anyone is watching, they'll think we've stopped for the night. But I want a messenger sent to Lord Cornwallis, so they'll be ready for us when we do arrive."

"Very good, Your Grace. I'll send Dibden." Dacre had told Harris to keep Dibden away from Christina, and the Captain thought this an excellent opportunity to remove him from her escort permanently. In five minutes, however, his aide came back. "I can't find Dibden anywhere, sir. He's supposed to be seeing to the horses, but they haven't seen him there." In an instant, Dacre was on his feet and running.

Christina had just bent over the woodpile when a hand closed over her mouth. Held in a brutal grip, her eyes met the small, burning eyes of Thomas Dibden. She tried to bite the hand that held her mouth so cruelly, but he only held her more tightly against him until her eyes were black with pain.

He was breathing heavily as he shifted his grip on her. The heavy hand left her mouth for just a minute and she cried out only to have her voice stifled by his mouth.

Desperately she fought with him. Her shirt ripped and his hands and mouth hurt cruelly. Christina was strong, but she was no match for the bull-like man who was so merciless in his attack.

Suddenly, Dibden's grip slackened and in a moment Christina found herself free. There was the sound of bone connecting with bone, and Dibden was flung in a heap on the pile of wood. The Duke stood over him, watching, but the man didn't move. He lay still, his neck bent at a curious angle. Dacre knelt next to him for a moment, his hand on Dibden's chest, then he turned to Christina. Her hair hung loose about her shoulders, her shirt was ripped, and her lip cut. They looked at each other, and suddenly something primitive and dangerous was in the air. With difficulty, Dacre spoke, "He's dead."

Her eyes never left the Duke. "Good," she replied huskily.

Dacre took a step toward her, then they heard the voice of Captain Harris. "Is everything all right, Your Grace?" The Captain, short of breath from running, came up between them, followed by several other soldiers.

If Dacre was breathing quickly also, Captain Harris put it down to exertion. The Duke's voice was calm enough when he answered. "I discovered Dibden trying to attack Lady Christina."

Shocked, the eyes of the soldiers turned to her. "Is this true, Lady Christina?" asked Harris.

"Yes." Suddenly Christina began to tremble uncontrollably. "He tried to...." She reached out for something to grab on to and found herself lifted up into Dacre's arms.

"I'll take Lady Christina back to her quarters," he said authoritatively, and without waiting for a reply,

38

bore her off. He kicked open the door of her room and, still holding her in his arms, sat down on the bed. She was shaking violently. "It's all right now, Christina," he said, his voice surprisingly gentle. He smoothed her loose hair back from her face. "You're safe."

It was too much. All the fear and tension of the last week, pent up so bravely, broke loose at his comforting words. She turned her head into his shoulder and wept. Her tears at first were harsh and difficult, the tears of someone who has had little practice crying. But soon their own momentum loosened them and released the floodgates.

Dacre held her, his heart torn by pity and some other emotion he didn't try to define. Her hair spilled through his fingers, spun silver in the dying light. Gradually her sobs slackened and she was quiet, her light bones lying still against him. She stayed so for a long minute, then raised her wet face and looked at him. "I'm sorry," she said in a low voice.

He took out his handkerchief and dried her cheeks in silence, his face unreadable save for the flicker of a muscle at the side of his mouth. He put the handkerchief back in his pocket, then, slowly, with the inevitability of tomorrow, he bent to touch her mouth with his. Her lips tasted of the salt of blood and tears and were soft and innocent under his.

Afterward, Christina couldn't remember when that gentle kiss changed into something else. She only remembered the sudden wild surge of blood in her veins, the aching delight of his mouth against her mouth, against her breasts. It was the voice of Captain Harris at the closed door that pulled them apart.

"I have to file a report of this incident with the commander here, Your Grace," his words came through to them. "I would appreciate your assistance."

It took Dacre a minute to get his voice under control and when he did speak it was hoarse. "I'll be with you in a minute, Captain," he called, then turned his head again and looked at Christina. She hadn't moved from where she was lying on the bed, her hair spilled around her, her torn shirt hanging off her shoulders baring her beautiful body to the waist. Her eyes were smoky in her crystal-clear face and for a long moment they looked at each other, saying nothing.

Finally Dacre spoke, his voice still brittle from hard-controlled emotion. "I won't say I'm sorry, because I'm not."

"I think you had better go," she said, her voice a thread of its usual clear tone. He looked enormous standing in the doorway, his hair pale copper in the dim light of the room. He hesitated a moment, then turned and went out of the door.

He left a Christina profoundly shaken by her own reaction. Men had been falling in love with her since she was thirteen, but, glorified by position and by name, she had experienced no difficulty in retaining her remoteness. All her passion had been for her country. Until now. She lay still for a long time, her mind grappling with this frightening new complication, until, worn out by emotion, she fell asleep.

The Duke, however, got little sleep that night. He had been attracted by Christina MacCarthy since their initial meeting, but he too had been unprepared for the extraordinary nature of what had suddenly blazed up between them. Like it or not, their relationship had been drastically altered by those few minutes in her room. And, in the look they had exchanged before he left, she had acknowledged that she knew this, too.

Chapter Four

O curlew, cry no more in the air,
Or only to the water in the west;
Because your crying brings to my mind
Passion-dimmed eyes and long heavy hair
That was shaken out over my breast:
There is enough evil in the crying of the
    wind.

—William Butler Yeats

The morning was damp and foggy, but it brought the strength of sober reflection to Christina. The event of last night she must resolutely push to the farthest recesses of her mind. That something of profound significance had happened between them, she acknowledged. But, with all her brain clearly focused on what lay before her, she resolved to ignore it.

The Duke found, as they rode side by side through the foggy countryside, that an invisible barrier had arisen between them. It was not the withdrawn silence of the earlier part of their journey; on the contrary, Christina threw up between them a constant flow of talk. And her topic was the one subject that more surely than anything else would be cause for a permanent division between them: Ireland. She took special pains to point out the poverty that surrounded them on every side. "This is the reality of Ireland, my lord Duke," she told him. "It is not fine country homes like the Clonmel's, or the elegance of Dublin drawing rooms. It is mud-walled cabins, bare-footed peasants, the reek of wet turf on the hearth as men, women, pigs, and chickens all huddle together for warmth. It is a hard place, for hard people."

"I can see that, Lady Christina," his voice was even and uninflected. "But what do you propose be done to correct it?"

Startled, she looked at him directly for the first time. "What do you mean?"

"You tried rebellion, and you failed. Have you any other plans?"

Her eyes, North Atlantic gray, looked bleakly into his. "My father tried every means possible, Your Grace, before resorting to violence. It was like whispering into a hurricane."

"He was dealing with the Irish Parliament. You may find the Parliament of the United Kingdom more receptive." She gestured helplessly, but he only said, "Think about it, Lady Christina. Going to prison will help no one."

"I didn't think I had a choice," she said tartly.

"Perhaps you do," he said enigmatically, and rode forward to speak to Captain Harris, leaving her with a frown between her clearly-marked brows.

Soon afterward they halted for a break of several hours. Dacre's place beside her had been taken by Captain Harris, and it was he who explained to Christina their decision to enter Dublin late at night. "There'll be no one around then to see us going to the Castle," he told her.

"The Castle?" Her voice was breathless. "Am I not to be taken to Kilmainham Gaol?"

"No, my lady. You're to be lodged at the Castle—at least until you can be brought to trial."

"I see." Her barely audible words were not an accurate reflection of the distress this news brought her. She had always assumed she would be taken to Kilmainham, the prison which had held Wolfe Tone and now held a number of veterans of the Rebellion. She had counted on the notorious freedom of Kilmainham to be able to talk to a few people—to Murdoch Lynch, in particular, a devoted follower of her father who had been in Kilmainham for two years now. Dacre had asked her today what her plans were for Ireland's future; she hadn't told him, but that was precisely what she wanted to talk to Murdoch about. For a year and a half she had been an outlaw in the remote mountains of the west. She needed to know where things stood with the United Irishmen movement. But her chances of talking to anyone except the English while incarcerated in Dublin Castle were slender.

It was a very quiet and sober Christina who rode beside Dacre as they approached Dublin late that night. She hadn't realized herself how much she had been relying on seeing Murdoch—her last link with her father. It was dark and cold and the English soldiers rode in tight formation around her as they clattered through the narrow streets of Dublin. For the first time in a number of days Christina found herself afraid. It was with effort that she kept her face expressionless as they rode into the Castle yard and Dacre helped her to dismount. The garrison had been waiting for them, and a soldier escorted them immediately to the Bermingham Tower, where so many Irish patriots, from Red Hugh O'Donnell on down, had been lodged before.

She was taken to a room on the upper floor, large and cold and barren. The huge door had an iron lock on it, and her gaze moved from the lock to the grimly barred windows. She drove her nails into her palms and instinctively turned to Dacre, her eyes unable to hide her rising panic.

His face was as bleak as her surroundings, but his voice was familiar and steady and helped to stem the tide of her fear. "Try to get some sleep," he told her. "I'll be back in the morning, with a few more amenities." His green eyes flickered around the barren room and came back to rest once more on her face. She looked more composed and even managed a smile.

"It's all right," she said. He nodded and, having seen that the soldier had provided her with candles and had lit the fire, he left. Christina slept better than he did that night.

He went to see Cornwallis immediately after breakfast the next morning. "I am glad to see you, Your Grace," the Lord Lieutenant greeted him. "How was the journey? I expected you sooner."

"I moved as fast as I could, my lord," Dacre said. "I did not like the temper of the countryside at all. Everywhere, but especially in the west, crowds of people came out to see Lady Christina. She is a heroine who is rapidly assuming the proportions of a martyr."

"I know," Cornwallis said gloomily. "I told you as much before you went to Kerry. She has become a symbol of national resistance, and the fact that she is a woman only increases her danger. This is, after all, a Catholic country."

"Lord Clonmel told me she is regarded as a secular version of the Virgin Mary."

"I very much fear he is right." Cornwallis arose from

44

his chair and went to look out the window. The Bermingham Tower was in full view and it was with his eyes on that grim building that Cornwallis spoke. "Now that we have her, Your Grace, what are we going to do with her?"

"That is what I wish to speak to you about, my lord. As you know, I intervened on the King's request that Lady Christina's life be spared. But I do not think that bringing her to trial is the answer to the problem she poses."

Cornwallis shuddered. "Certainly not. It would only inflame the people—perhaps to the point of rebellion. It would be ironic if she succeeded in doing from prison what she could not do in the field." Cornwallis turned from the window to regard the still figure of Dacre seated at the beautifully carved table which held the Marquis's books. "We need to get her out of the country, Your Grace. Permanently, if possible."

Dacre's eyes were on the finely-tooled leather volume he held in his strong, slender fingers and his deep voice was even and unhurried as he agreed with Cornwallis. "King Ludwig wants his granddaughter in Letzau, I understand. When I undertook this mission our purpose was to offer Lady Christina the same option granted to the other United Irishmen leaders: Freedom upon her promise to permanently exile herself to the country of her choice. Her grandfather would receive her with royal fanfare in Letzau."

The tense Dacre had used did not escape Cornwallis. "Your purpose 'was,' Your Grace? What has changed?"

Dacre finally looked up from his book, and his eyes, brilliantly green, met Cornwallis's. "I do not think she will go," he said simply.

Cornwallis stared back at him tensely. "Why not?"

The deep, even voice did not alter. "I believe she feels it her duty to remain in Ireland."

Cornwallis looked again toward the Bermingham Tower. "Are you sure?"

"No." Dacre rose to his feet. "And I think we should give her time to reflect on the implications of her imprisonment before we make the offer. She was deeply upset to hear she was going to the Castle and not Kilmainham. Probably she had counted on contacting someone there. I think we should keep her isolated from anyone who might bring her news of rebel plans. If she feels helpless and, most of all, if she feels useless, she might agree to exile."

Cornwallis nodded slowly. "I'll see to it, Your Grace. But I understand you ordered books and clothes to be sent to her. Is not that undermining your own plan?"

Dacre walked to the door. "After a year and a half of guerrilla warfare in the mountains of Kerry, I doubt if physical discomfort would weigh in any decision Lady Christina made. If she thought that she would be of more assistance to her country in exile than she would be in prison, then she might agree. But we need to keep her isolated."

"We will, Your Grace," promised the Lord Lieutenant.

The days and weeks went by. Dacre went to see Christina once, the day after they arrived in Dublin, then left her alone. The only people who saw her during this time were a priest and a lawyer, both under the control of Dublin Castle. Dacre waged a constant battle with himself: The desire to see her warred with his knowledge that her ultimate safety depended upon her accepting exile. And that was a decision she needed time, and isolation, to come to.

He was busy. It was the death throes of Ireland's independent Parliament and Dublin was in a ferment. But Castlereagh and Cornwallis had done their jobs too well; there was little doubt as to the outcome of the coming vote. Only Henry Grattan, supported by a loyal few, continued to fight the overwhelming tide.

Dacre met Grattan on one very public occasion, and the result of that meeting sent shock waves around the close-knit Protestant Ascendancy. The occasion was an afternoon reception given by Lady Beresford for government members. Dacre looked in for a few minutes and was chatting to an immensely gratified hostess when Henry Grattan, also a surprise guest, approached them.

"I do not believe we have met, Your Grace," he said. Lady Beresford, her eyes wide with alarm, introduced the two men. "I hope you are satisfied, Your Grace, with the results of your policy here in Ireland." Grattan's voice shook with emotion.

"Which aspect of that policy do you refer to, Mr. Grattan?" The Duke's voice was impeccably courteous.

"The purchase of the Irish Parliament is what I refer to, Duke."

Dacre raised an eyebrow. "I don't think I understand you, Mr. Grattan," he said pleasantly.

"Then let me make myself quite clear. I charge you publicly, my lord Duke, with making corrupt offers of peerages in order to sway votes; I charge you with bribing members of the house to vacate their seats in order to fill them with servants of the Castle, I charge you with corrupting the assembly of the people...."

"What people, Mr. Grattan?" The Duke's voice was more clipped than usual. He looked from his splendid height on the frail, sickly form of Henry Grattan. The room was suddenly silent, listening tensely to the two men.

Grattan was brought up short, then answered clearly. "The Irish people, Your Grace."

"Spare me your rhetoric, Mr. Grattan." The Duke spoke softly, but his voice was perfectly audible to the whole room. "Seventy-five percent of the Irish people are Roman Catholics and, as such, are not allowed to sit in the 'assembly of the people,' as you call it. The Irish Parliament is the bastion of an elite Protestant society which is interested, not in the people of Ireland, but in retaining its own special privileges. I have just taken a trip across the country and seen with my own eyes the condition of the Irish people under your sacred Parliament. They live on the extreme verge of human misery. In all of Europe I have not seen a peasantry so destitute."

Grattan's eyes fell. He had fought, unavailingly, for the reform of Parliament and the rights of Catholics. He spoke slowly, "What you say is true, Your Grace, to my sorrow. But if a resident Parliament and resident gentry cannot improve matters, will no Parliament and fewer gentry do it?"

Dacre's deep voice was mercilessly clear to the whole room. "Do you people even begin to realize what a powder keg you are sitting on? You have a whole nation of souls here, dispossessed, desperate, and living solely on potatoes. Something obviously has to be done, and as it cannot be done in Dublin, it will have to be done in London."

There was a strange look in Grattan's eyes. "Does the rest of Mr. Pitt's government feel this way, Your Grace?"

Dacre smiled and, in spite of himself, Grattan felt the muscles in his face relax. "We shall soon see, Mr. Grattan," he said gently. Shortly after, he made his departure, leaving a feeling of distinct uneasiness behind him.

During these weeks of waiting, reports had been trickling in of trouble in the west. As the days went by, however, the agitation began to accelerate and to spread. Cattle were driven into the sea, and agents received notes saying "Free Christina MacCarthy."

Some Protestant churches were fired and graves were dug before Protestant homes. On the day of Dacre's historic confrontation with Henry Grattan, he received an urgent summons from the Lord Lieutenant. He found Cornwallis pacing the floor of his office. "They've set fire to Clonmel House, Your Grace." He swung around and flung out his hands at Dacre. "We must do something about her!"

Dacre looked suddenly weary. "I know, Lord Cornwallis. I don't think we need to worry about any organized rising, but isolated terrorist activity can be almost as bad."

"This damn country," Cornwallis grumbled. "If the landlords only behaved with common decency toward their tenants, none of this kind of thing would happen."

"I know," Dacre repeated.

"Will you see Lady Christina and see if you can get her to accept exile?"

"Yes," Dacre said, his deep voice more clipped than usual. "I will see her immediately."

Christina was seated at the simple table in her room, her eyes fixed uncomprehendingly on a book, when she heard the sound of feet on the stairs and then the key in the lock. She turned, saw him in the doorway, and felt a pain constrict her chest, as if her whole breathing apparatus had just shut down.

Dacre's face had radically altered at the sight of her. She was thinner than he remembered, her cheekbones too sharp in her white face. But her hair was the same spill of moonlight, her gray eyes as clear under the grave, beautiful brow.

Those eyes met his and the room was suddenly charged with tension. It was out in the open again, not just sexual attraction, though certainly that was there, but the acknowledgment of a bond so powerful

49

it was almost tangible. Finally, Christina wrenched her eyes away and looked at her hands, gripped together in her lap. "Why are you here?" she asked harshly.

He looked at her hands as well; the wrists were too bony as they protruded from the sleeves of her new wool dress. "Aren't you eating?" he asked, his voice brittle with stifled emotion.

"It is not food that I'm hungry for," she said briefly. "Why am I being held in isolation like this? When is my trial? I demand to see my own lawyer."

He came slowly into the room and sat down on the edge of the table. "I have been waiting to hear from the Prime Minister before I saw you," he said carefully. "I am now in receipt of his letter authorizing me to offer terms to you. If you will agree to exile yourself to a country of your choice, the government will set you free." As she said nothing, he continued, "When King Ludwig first wrote to his Majesty King George, he urgently requested that you be allowed to go to Letzau. The King wishes to honor his request."

She looked at him, her gray eyes open and without light. "When is my trial set for?" she said tonelessly.

He spoke with a weariness she could just hear. "There will be no trial, Christina. Surely you know that by now. The Habeas Corpus Act is suspended in Ireland. You will be held, without trial, indefinitely."

"God help me," she said, in a voice so low he could barely hear it.

He leaned forward and spoke urgently. "Go to your grandfather, Christina. We are on the verge of enacting the Union of our two countries. When we meet as one Parliament in Westminster, I promise you I will work for Catholic Emancipation and for land reform. It is necessary—that is obvious to me; and it will be made clear to the Parliament. Give the Union a chance to work for you. Go to Letzau."

"I can't," she said simply.

His mouth set in hard lines. "Christ, you're stubborn," he said. "What good can you possibly do sitting here in prison that you couldn't do, free, in Letzau?"

"I'm Irish, Duke," she said. "I know the value of a symbol. And that is what I am. What good can I do my people? None, if I leave. If I stay, I at least demonstrate that they are not alone and that it is always possible to say no. You may imprison me, but you can't imprison the spirit of resistance I symbolize."

"I thought you didn't want any more blood shed."

"I don't. Not Irish blood, at any rate."

"Aren't you inviting just that?"

"I don't know. I only know I can't leave. I can't," she repeated helplessly, "not when things are as bad as they are. You wouldn't understand."

He walked to the window and put his hand on the iron bars. "Oddly enough, I do understand," he said harshly. "But I don't like it. Lost causes have never had any appeal for me."

She smiled faintly. "That's because you're English. I'm Irish. I was brought up on them." Her eyes went past him to the barred window, bathed now with bright sun. The smells of dust and horses and life were wafted into the room on a soft breeze. "Is it possible for me to be allowed to take some exercise?" she asked breathlessly.

At the look on her face he felt like smashing his fist into the stone wall. "I'll see about it," he grated. "And think about what I just said. The offer still stands if you change your mind. And I will honor my promise to work for reforms in Parliament."

"I won't change my mind."

"Then God help you."

"I hope He will," she answered soberly. "I need Him."

Dacre had to report failure to Cornwallis, and as the final weeks of May went by, the unrest in the country accelerated. Burnings and animal destruction spread from the west to the rest of the counties. When two hundred of the Earl of Clare's prime cattle were driven over a cliff into the sea, the pressures on Cornwallis to "do something" about Christina MacCarthy became even stronger.

"Our choices in regard to Lady Christina are rather limited," Dacre pointed out to Cornwallis when the Marquis had sought him out after a particularly scalding meeting with Lord Clare. "She will not give us any guarantees if we send her to Letzau, so that if we do release her to her grandfather she will probably be back in Ireland within a month. We could bring her to trial, but that would only give her a public forum to castigate us. The King won't hear of the death penalty, so all we could do is imprison her again. We can hold her indefinitely without trial, in the hopes that public fury will wear itself out. Have you any other suggestions, my lord?" Dacre's voice was steady and uninflected; nothing showed in either his face or his voice to indicate that the fate of Christina MacCarthy was anything more to him than a thorny political problem.

"All I know, Your Grace, is that the bloody girl is more trouble now that she is in prison than she ever was running free. Can we at least get her out of Ireland?"

Dacre looked at his long, elegant hands. "I suppose so. I was planning to leave shortly for England; I want to discuss this whole situation with Mr. Pitt personally. Perhaps I will take Lady Christina with me. At least we will have put the Irish Sea between her and her ferocious countrymen."

Cornwallis looked distinctly relieved. "The idea of

an English prison might even pressure Lady Christina into changing her mind about exile."

A muscle tightened beside Dacre's mouth, but otherwise his expression remained unruffled. "Nothing is going to change Lady Christina's mind, Lord Cornwallis."

"No, I suppose not." Cornwallis spoke with grudging admiration. "She is a very determined woman, Lady Christina, and a very brave one. And, Your Grace, I want her off my hands!"

"Very well." Dacre rose to his feet and ushered Cornwallis to the door. "I will write to Mr. Pitt to say I am escorting Lady Christina to England. What happens next will be up to the Prime Minister."

Chapter Five

O my eagle!
Why do you beat vain wings upon the rock
When hollow night's above?
—William Butler Yeats

On June 7, 1800, a Bill of Union was passed by the Irish Parliament. Ireland would no longer have a parliament of her own; from now on she was to be governed from London. On June 8, Charles Standish, Duke of Dacre and Home Secretary of the British government, left Dublin to escort Lady Christina MacCarthy to London.

Christina had thought long and hard after hearing from Dacre that he was to take her to England. Not for trial; he had made it perfectly clear that the Government would never give her the public stage of a trial.

"It is a splendid union you are offering us, Duke,"

she had said. "Full participation in the blessings of the English constitution, did you say? Is not habeas corpus a part of that same constitution? Are any Englishmen in fear of prison without trial, or does that honor fall only to the Irish?"

"I know, Lady Christina," he had said shortly. "But Pitt will never agree to a trial, And, for you, the result would be the same."

"Prison."

"Yes."

"At least I would have a chance to hold England up before the eyes of the Christian world as the destroyer she is."

"That is precisely why you will not be given a trial."

She thought of that conversation now as she stood on the deck of the ship that was taking her from Ireland. Perpetual imprisonment was impossible for her. Her courage failed at few things, but it failed at the thought of passing the remainder of her life shut away from air and sky and converse with dear friends. Her decision had been made, and now, as she watched the shore receding before her, she felt at peace. Softly she murmured:

> *Tréide as dile lem for-ácbas*
> *Ar bith buidnech—*
> *Durmag, Doire, dinn ard ainglech is Tír*
> *Luigdech*
> *Ro grádriges íatha Éirenn deilm cen*
> *ellach....*

"What is that you are saying?" It was Dacre's deep voice as he came to stand beside her at the rail.

"It's an ancient Irish poem. It says, 'I have left the three things I love best in the populated world—Durrow, Derry, that home of angels, and Tir Luigdech. I say in truth, I have loved the lands of Ireland....'" Her voice trailed away as her eyes remained fixed on the now-distant shore.

Dacre turned to look at her as she stood beside him in the bright sunshine. She wore the peat-colored cloak he had bought for her and her hair was simply braided into a coronet on top of her head. She looked thinner than ever, and too clear, as if burning with an inner fire.

"I wish I had met you under any circumstances but these," he said somberly.

She didn't pretend not to understand him. "It wouldn't be any good, no matter what the circumstances," she said. "You are English and I am Irish. That is a gulf we could never bridge."

"Is it so impossible for our two countries ever to live together in peace?"

She laughed shortly. "To an Irishman, Your Grace, there is only one word for an Englishman: enemy. Have you forgotten the penal laws? We have not. Under those laws no Irish Catholic could attend mass, go to school, hold public office, engage in trade or commerce, purchase land, lease land, be guardian to a child, et cetera, et cetera. They were intended to make us poor, ignorant, and servile."

She turned to look at him now and leaned closer in her intensity. "Some of us survived that dark age better than others. The MacCarthys were lucky; we kept our land, we smuggled our children to France for an education, and we smuggled our wool to France for good profits. So, because we retained our property, our money, and our education, we owe something to those who did not." Her eyes, gravely intent, searched his profile. It looked like a mask in bronze, brutally composed. The sun struck sparks of gold from his hair and the glimmer of green fire from beneath his lashes. There was a long pause, then he said, in a carefully neutral voice, "Your father and mine must have graduated from the same school."

"What do you mean?" she asked quietly.

"I mean that I have heard that speech before," he said. "Or a variation of it. Just before my father died, I had told him I wanted to go to South America on a geological expedition with Alexander von Humboldt. He read me much the same speech you just gave; the one that dwelt on my duty to my country and my responsibilities as a Standish."

"Have your family always been in government?"

"Since the fourteenth century, according to my aunts."

"And do you like it?"

"The ability to rule was bred into my bones and into my brains," he answered, "as it was into yours. One always likes what one is good at. But," and now he turned to face her directly, "I don't like this. And I don't know what to do about it."

There was sympathy for him in her clear gray eyes. "It is always easier, morally, to be the victim than it is to be the conqueror," she said softly.

He turned abruptly and went back into the cabin, leaving Christina alone on the deck, with the devastating sympathy still in her eyes.

She stayed on deck for the entire trip. "I shall be indoors again soon enough," she told Dacre when he asked if she wanted to come in out of the glare of the sun; and he had not asked her again.

He rejoined her about an hour before they landed. "We shall spend the night in port," he said, "and leave for London in the morning."

She nodded acquiescence, her eyes on the changing sky. "Don't you even want to know where you are going?" he asked impatiently.

"The Tower, I expect," she answered peacefully.

57

He looked at her serene profile and his mouth took on the grim lines so familiar to it these days. "What do you have in mind to do, Christina?" he asked imperatively.

She smiled. "What can I do, Your Grace? I thought simply, I might translate some poetry."

His face did not alter. "I see."

"I have always wanted to translate the story of Cuchulain." Suddenly she was deadly serious, feeling that somehow he must understand what she was planning to do. If he understood, perhaps he would forgive. "Cuchulain is our great national hero," she said slowly, "the Achilles, Lancelot, and Roland of our literature. The greatest of the stories surrounding him deals with his death."

"I have never heard of him." He caught the urgency of her mood, but was mystified by its cause. "Tell me about him," he said.

She leaned her arms upon the ship's rail and, eyes on the water, spoke in the cadences of the seanachie, or professional storyteller, from whom she had heard the tale. "Cuchulain was the chief warrior of the ancient kingdom of Ulster. The King of Ulster at this time was called Conchubor and his capital was at Emain Macha.

"There are many stories about Cuchulain: how Maeve, queen of Connaught, stole a prize bull and fought a war over it with Cuchulain and the Red Branch warriors of Ulster; how he killed his only son and in grief went out to fight the sea. But the greatest tale of all is the manner of his death. Maeve, Cuchulain's ancient enemy, was coming north again with a great army to invade and destroy Ulster. Cuchulain was on his way to meet her when messages arrived from Conchubar that the King's army would not arrive in time to aid him. Cuchulain had fought Maeve single handedly before and he went now to do so again.

"The battle was fierce and Cuchulain killed many men and forced them to retreat. But in the fight Cuchulain received his own death wound. He lashed himself against a stone pillar with his belt so that he might meet death on his feet. He remained so for a long time, with the circling army afraid to approach him for fear he was still alive. It was not until a vulture came and perched on his shoulder that they moved, for then they knew that Cuchulain was truly dead."

"And did the army of the king arrive then?" Dacre asked.

"Yes. And Ulster was saved."

He was silent for a long time, moved and obscurely frightened. What was she trying to tell him with this strange tale of lonely sacrifice and death?

"We are landing." Her voice, brisk and prosaic, destroyed the mood she herself had created. "Do you know, my lord Duke, that this will be the first time I have ever set a foot on English soil?"

And so once again he escorted Christina MacCarthy to prison. This time it was the Tower of London, words to strike terror into the heart of anyone coming into its shadow as a captive. But Christina showed no fear; her face was bright as a torch and her eyes rested on him as they said good-bye with an odd mixture of sorrow and sympathy.

"You will be comfortable enough," he told her. "Have patience. I will try to work things out."

"Yes." Her voice was muted. "May I see a priest? A priest of my own?"

"Send for whom you want. I'll see it cleared."

Her brow was perfectly clear as she smiled at him. "Don't come to see me. It doesn't help."

"No." He found his breathing was beginning to play tricks on him and with a tremendous effort of will he cleared his vision. "I won't come until I can offer you your freedom," he said.

The silver-blond head nodded gravely and he realized that he was expected to go. "Wait for me," he said, and she didn't seem to find his words odd.

"I will try," she said. "Good-bye—Charles."

She gave him two weeks. During that time Dacre moved heaven and earth to get the government to release her but, as he had known before he started, to no avail.

His first interview with the Prime Minister showed him clearly enough how things stood. Pitt looked very ill when Dacre arrived at Downing Street, but his expression lightened somewhat at the sight of Dacre's tall, commanding figure. "Have you heard the news, Your Grace?" he demanded immediately.

The Duke raised his eyebrows. "What news, Mr. Pitt?"

"Napoleon's victory at Marengo."

"When?"

"A week ago. Bonaparte has now undisputed control of France and northern Italy."

Dacre cautiously lowered his big frame into one of the fragile chairs in the room. "If Austria has been beaten, our coalition is finished. We will have to sue for peace."

The lines in Pitt's face became, if possible, even deeper. "The Cabinet is deeply divided over the issue of peace or war. God knows what will happen now."

Dacre drew on the reserves of discipline and courtesy he always needed when dealing with the Prime Minister and most of his colleagues. With lucid, passionless economy, he laid before Pitt the problems surrounding the capture of Christina MacCarthy.

When Dacre had finished, Pitt laced his fingers together and leaned toward the Duke. "In your judgment, Your Grace, how dangerous was the unrest in Ireland?"

"Dangerous enough. If there is a general uprising throughout the nation, we won't be able to control it. The French would love to have Ireland as a base of operations against us."

"Will executing her solve the problem?"

Dacre's gaze, faintly hostile, was level on the Prime Minister's face. "It would, I suspect, be just what is needed to provoke open rebellion."

Pitt rubbed his forehead. "Damn the girl! Then all we can do is keep her locked up and hope the situation cools down of its own accord."

"There is another possibility."

Pitt's head jerked up. "What is that, Your Grace?"

"I suggest we set her free," said Dacre.

"What!"

"We have just contracted a political union of our two kingdoms, Mr. Pitt. What better time to demonstrate that we no longer consider Ireland a hostile country, but part of our own nation. If we release Christina MacCarthy, we will be making a gesture of incalculable value." An austere smile crossed Dacre's face. "Lady Christina herself told me that the Irish are always ready to respond to a symbol. The best way to defuse her is to release her."

A deep frown creased Pitt's forehead. "There may be truth in what you say, Duke, but the Protestant leaders in Ireland would never stand for it. Her release may or may not quiet the Catholic rebellion, but it would most certainly provoke the Protestants!"

Dacre's face was unreadable. "And in all cases of conflicting needs, we always support the Protestants, do we not?"

"At least they are loyal, Your Grace."

"Why wouldn't they be?" Dacre returned. "The slave-

owner is always loyal to the state that perpetrates slav-
ery."

As the door closed behind Dacre, Pitt was left to
wonder just what the Duke had meant by that last
remark. All he was sure of was that he did not like it.

Chapter Six

> "I will not be clapped in a hood,
> Nor a cage, nor alight upon wrist,
> Now I have learnt to be proud
> Hovering over the wood
> In the broken mist
> Or tumbling cloud."
>
> —William Butler Yeats

Dacre went through the entire Cabinet in his efforts to free Christina. Aside from his admittedly personal interest in the results, her release was obviously the only solution to an impossible situation. Dacre had never been overly impressed by the astuteness of the government ministers; their lack of imagination and forethought in this affair he found nothing short of harrowing. But neither logic nor conscience could move them. Simply, they were afraid of the reaction of the Protestant Ascendancy.

After ten days, Dacre gave up and left London. Ostensibly, he was going to Manchester to deal with a potential riot. The war with France had drained national resources; there were serious food shortages in many parts of England and an ugly situation had developed in Manchester. In reality, Dacre went because he needed time to think.

He spent three days in Manchester, then drove himself to his estate in Scotland. Two weeks later he arrived at Strands, his chief residence in Cumberland. He had been there a week when Pitt's messenger found him.

In his weeks of absence Dacre had come to a possible solution to his problem. But, in order for it to be successful, additional pressure would have to be brought to bear on the English government. That that additional pressure was being applied was clear from Pitt's urgent message. But the news caused Dacre to be swept by such icy fury and stark terror that for long moments he was incapable of speech. Precisely twenty minutes after reading Pitt's letter he was in his phaeton and on his way to London.

Christina had taken matters into her own hands. To the dismay of the English Government, she was fasting to death in the Tower of London.

By the time Dacre reached London, Christina's fast was four weeks old, and the British Cabinet was badly frightened. The reports from Ireland were harrowing. Violence was erupting all over the country. What was most disturbing to Dublin Castle was the degree of organization behind the violence. "There is an embryonic nationalist movement in the making here," Cornwallis had written to Pitt. "If it is not halted immediately, I cannot answer for the consequences."

Dacre went to Westminster immediately after he arrived in London. As soon as Pitt saw his tall figure in the Peer's Gallery, he left the floor. Dacre joined him and they proceded to the government office.

Dacre sat in a chair by the window. The July sun was warm on his burnished gold head; his face was as calm and arrogant as ever. He had been preparing for this interview during the whole furious drive back from Strands; now that the moment had come his brain was icily clear, his determination unshakable. He opened the game by going on the offensive immediately. "What do you plan to do about Lady Christina?" he asked Pitt.

The Prime Minister looked grim. "I was hoping you might have some suggestions, Your Grace. To be frank, I don't know what to do. I have been to see her personally. I begged her to go to her grandfather. I even said we would accept her verbal word of honor not to engage in treasonable activities. She would not even have to promise not to return to Ireland!"

"And?"

"She refused." Pitt slammed his hand on his desk. "Why is she doing this, Dacre? Will she really go through with it?"

"We have given her no alternative, Mr. Pitt. Perpetual imprisonment would be worse than death to a temperament like Lady Christina's. And the terms we have offered for her freedom are impossible for her to honorably accept. She once said to me of her people 'If my death would help them, I'd go to it gladly.' Yes, I would say she means to go through with it."

"It wouldn't be so bad if she were just an ordinary rebel. But she's related to royalty all over Europe. I've had formal protests from three German states, and from Denmark. And Cornwallis writes that Ireland is on fire."

Dacre rose from his chair, his tall figure blocking the window, his short hair bright gold in the sun. "The Rebellion of ninety-eight thrust Christina MacCarthy into the role of leadership and left her there, the only native Irish chief who refused to bow to the enemy. Her power is the power of a symbol. This she knows. Her fast is an act of courage, made in cold blood and clear knowledge of its significance. It is also, I believe, an act of desperation, taken because she quite simply had no alternative. If we offer her an alternative, she may take it. Or she may not."

Pitt looked at him intently. "What can we feasibly offer her, Your Grace?"

"To satisfy Lady Christina we must release her with no promises on her part about her future behavior. To satisfy the government, to save our face as it were, we need some kind of guarantee about her future loyalty."

"The two conditions are mutually exclusive, I am afraid."

"Not necessarily," Dacre said slowly. "Someone else might stand surety for Lady Christina."

"Who?"

No sign of tension marred the calm surface of Dacre's face. "I will, Mr. Pitt."

There was a long silence, then the Prime Minister asked carefully, "And how do you propose to do that, Your Grace?"

"If Lady Christina were my wife, she would be under my constant observation. If she were released as the Duchess of Dacre, I do not think there would be many repercussions, Mr. Pitt. There are few people who would doubt my loyalty."

"Are you proposing to marry Lady Christina, Dacre?" the Prime Minister asked incredulously.

"I am."

Pitt shook his head as if the motion would clear his brain. "Do you think Lady Christina will agree?"

Dacre looked rueful. "I don't know, Mr. Pitt. I hope so."

Pitt sat in thought for several minutes, then looked

up. "I think it will do. If she agrees, all I can say is thank you, Your Grace. You will have relieved us of a major difficulty."

Dacre looked briefly amused. "I wonder, Mr. Pitt," he said. "I will go directly to the Tower and communicate with you as soon as I have seen Lady Christina. If she agrees, I want her removed from there immediately."

"The sooner the better," the Prime Minister agreed fervently. "I wish you luck, Your Grace."

Dacre drove immediately to the Tower of London, stopping only to pick up his personal physician. He had no intention of allowing Christina the luxury of her sacrifice. He did not think she had cast herself willingly in the role of Cuchulain, but once having embraced the part he feared she might be unwilling to renounce it. If he had to remove her by force, he was prepared to do so. There was, however, another factor operating in the situation that was not at all political, and Dacre hoped the power of the undeniable relationship that existed between them would be a decided factor in what was to happen next.

He left the doctor in his carriage in the courtyard in front of the chapel and went with the sergeant who was in charge of Christina up the stairs to her prison door. The soldier unlocked the door and Dacre said calmly, "If you will wait below, sergeant, I shall call when I need you." The man nodded briefly and descended the stairs, leaving Dacre alone on the landing.

It was a few moments before he opened the door and entered her room. The room was silent and seemingly empty and Dacre walked swiftly to the center, raking the bare stone walls with his eyes before he saw the slight figure on the narrow bed. He dropped down beside her, his eyes on her sleeping face, so thin and white on the rough pillow. Its beautiful bones were mercilessly clear under the flesh, and her figure looked painfully thin under her clothes. He looked at her hand, that capable boy's hand he had noticed so many weeks ago; it looked nearly transparent. He reached out his own strong fingers and covered it. It seemed a long time before the long lashes fluttered and opened. "Who is it?" she said, in a weak voice.

"Charles," he answered.

"Charles." Her lips formed the word though no sound came. Her great hollow eyes clung to his face, and he remained perfectly still, afraid to fracture her tenuous hold on consciousness. Finally, "You came," she said.

"I was out of town and did not know. I came as soon as I heard." He leaned closer. "I keep my promises, Christina. I have come to offer you your freedom."

Her gaze drifted away from his. "You can't," she said faintly. "I won't accept it." Her lip curled slightly and a flicker of light stirred in the blackness of her eyes. "Pitt came to see me. He was afraid."

"He is afraid," said Dacre frankly. "And so am I. For you. I won't deny that your actions have made an impact, but another armed rising in Ireland will only meet with the same result as all the others. You cannot beat us in the field, Christina. You know that."

She did not answer, her face turned away from his. "Christina!" he said imperatively, and she turned and looked at him. "Let me take this fight into Parliament. The time has come to see what the political process can do. Give up this fast, accept your freedom, and give England a chance to keep faith."

Deep distress was stamped on her wasted face. "I cannot promise...."

"You won't have to promise anything," he cut in.

She stared at him, her eyes enormous. He went on, his even voice only slightly deeper than usual. "In order for you to leave here a free woman, you need

68

promise nothing to the English government. They will release you unequivocally. I am afraid, however, there is one catch." He had her undivided attention, her eyes great dark pools fixed on his face. "You must marry me."

The silence was shattering. He could feel her surprise like a physical thing. As she continued to remain silent, he added slowly. "Marry me, and I will promise you to work for Catholic Emancipation and for land reform. If I fail, you will be free to go back to Ireland and take whatever actions you feel are necessary."

Christina felt a pain deep within her, and turned her eyes away from him. She had gone a long way on her journey and death loomed now more as friend than enemy. She did not want to turn back, and the slight negative motion of her head on the pillow told Dacre of her feelings.

Without compunction he spoke her name again and caught and held her eyes with his merciless green gaze. He trained on her slight, vulnerable figure all the concentrated power of his determination, fine-boned and ruthless in its effect.

"I can't," she said once, helplessly.

"You can and you will," he answered, his voice matter-of-fact and definite. Their eyes met and held once more, and this time the level of their communication was very different from what had been between them up until now.

Time ceased. The next sound in the room was the low tones of Christina's voice as she answered the very personal question that now lay between them. "All right," she said, "I will marry you, Charles."

The doctor was sent for and, after a brief examination, Christina was conveyed to Dacre House in Grosvenor Square. Dacre sent a message to Pitt saying he was taking Lady Christina to Strands and would be away for several weeks. Then he set about procuring a special license and finding the priest who had been Christina's confessor to perform the marriage ceremony. They were married the next morning and left shortly after for Strands, the Duke's main seat in Cumberland.

Chapter Seven

O love is the crooked thing,
There is nobody wise enough
To find out all that is in it.
                    —William Butler Yeats

For Christina, the first week of her marriage was just a series of brief vignettes interspersed with sleep.

She remembered the red dusk and the smell of the trees as she left the Tower carried in Dacre's arms. She remembered the feel of his coat under her cheek and the irresistible feeling of safety and strength his closeness gave her.

She remembered the bedroom at Dacre House and the thin face of the doctor. She remembered Dacre's face as he coaxed food down her throat and the kind face of the housekeeper who undressed her and put her to bed.

She remembered the brief ceremony and the worried face of Father Connolly. She had smiled reassurance at him and he had surprisingly kissed her hand.

The journey north was a clouded memory also, becoming confused in her mind with the other journeys she had taken with Dacre. He was conscious of her weakness and confusion, and dealt with her very gently. He was careful to keep his talk to simple things, the country they were passing through, his home at Strands, childhood memories. Never did he mention Ireland or the recent political upheavals that had brought them together.

Some words of his she remembered vividly, because they cast a new light on him and so had captured her wandering attention. As the chaise had moved out of Kendal, Dacre had begun to talk about his home. "I think it was growing up here that got me interested in geography. Cumberland is so clearly hewn from rock; the land cries out of a history of its own. The names here are Norwegian, you know. They come from the Vikings, who came from Iceland in the eleventh century."

He had looked out the window of the chaise at the blue-gray silhouette of peaks, glowing almost violet in the heat of the afternoon. "My father never could understand my interest in geography. But, then, he never liked Cumberland. He lived mostly in Sussex, in a house he had built by Robert Adam. It is a masterpiece, I believe. But I like Strands."

"Geography," she said faintly. "Do you ever regret letting your father talk you into giving up your expedition with von Humboldt?"

"Sometimes. It is a science that is changing enormously; for the first time it is being studied for its own sake, not just as an illustration of history. It's a temptation: to leave everything behind and embark on a trip to the wilds of tropical America or Russian Asia. At any rate, I helped to finance von Humboldt's expedition. And, on the whole, my father was probably right; my destiny lies here." His eyes had rested on the silver-fair head next to him as he spoke; nor was he referring to Westminster.

She remembered also her first view of Strands. They had turned west from Lake Grasmere and were proceding along a narrow, well-kept road when Dacre's hand touched her arm. "We're almost there," he said. The road turned into a wide, tree-lined drive which bordered on the sparkling waters of a mountain lake. They passed over a stone bridge and came into an open park. There, surrounded by green lawns and formal gardens, and backed by mountains, was Strands. It was large and sprawling, made of dark stone brightened by hundreds of window panes sparkling in the summer sun.

"It's an architectural monstrosity," Dacre said affectionately. "The original house was built in the time of Richard the Second and since then every owner has added something to it. Fortunately, they all used local stone, so there is some basic uniformity."

"I like it," she had said simply, and his hand had tightened momentarily on her arm.

Christina's arrival at Strands was an event long remembered by every servant who was present. The major-domo, Mr. Yeadon, had them all lined up in the hall, with himself and four footmen stationed on the steps in front of the great door. When the carriage drew up, the footmen went immediately to open the door and to assist the occupants to alight.

The Duke appeared first in the doorway of the coach, his hair bright in the July sun. He shook his head at the footmen, said something, and turned to help the Duchess out himself. Mr. Yeadon went to meet them and the three of them moved very slowly up the stairs and into the great hall where the staff was assembled.

Mrs. Ireby, the housekeeper who had virtually raised the Duke until he was old enough to be sent to school, moved forward and asked Christina if she would like to go right upstairs, but she shook her head and, with the unflagging courtesy that had been bred into her, allowed Mr. Yeadon to introduce each and every member of the great household.

Christina wore a traveling dress of pale blue which hung loosely on her too slender figure. Her face was pale and thin, her eyes the only spot of color about her. The thick silver hair was pulled softly off her wide brow and coiled simply at the back of her head. The staff, who had been prepared to resent this strange Irishwoman who was to be their new mistress, thought at first she was the most beautiful thing they had ever seen. They saw her obvious weakness, her scrupulous courtesy, and her grave smile. By the time Mrs. Ireby had escorted her upstairs, Christina had won her new title in the hearts as well as on the lips of the Strands staff.

Mrs. Ireby had been looking at the Duke as well as at Christina. What she saw in his face allayed any fears she might have had; the tense, strained look of his last, brief visit was gone, replaced by something Mrs. Ireby had never seen on his strong, arrogant features before. With genuine concern and deep satisfaction, Mrs. Ireby settled the new Duchess into the large, sunny bedroom that was to be hers. Everything, thought the housekeeper, had worked out for the best.

Dacre remained at Strands for another ten days. During that time, Christina slowly gained in physical strength, but mentally she seemed to be overcome by a deep listlessness that frightened Dacre. She was content, as long as he was by her, to just sit quietly in the sun, her eyes on the mountains or the flowers or the water. What was going on behind her serene gray gaze he didn't know. When he was absent she became restless, but still absorbed by the apathy he worried about.

It wasn't just the trauma of returning to life and health after such a close contact with death that was disturbing her. Dacre felt there was some trouble she had buried deep and, for some reason, was trying not to have to face. After ten days he judged she was physically strong enough to do without the crutch of his presence. Whatever was bothering her she would have to face alone.

She didn't protest at his going, but he knew she was distressed. Parliament was finishing up, and he had serious business to put before the Prime Minister. He simply told her he was going to make the first move in his strategy to get the Cabinet to consider a Catholic Emancipation Bill. He went into no details; she wasn't ready. Dacre was also finding it increasingly difficult to be so constantly close to her and to make no physical demands. But she wasn't ready for that, either. So he went.

London was sweltering. After the cool of the mountains, Dacre found it almost unbearably oppressive. But he had come with a definite purpose in mind, and now that Christina was safe he was free to give the whole of his formidable attention to it. He had promised her to do something for Ireland. More than that, he had himself come to the conclusion that political stability for England rested on a sound, working union with Ireland, and that union would only be effective if the Irish people were given some very substantial concessions.

He arrived in London on Wednesday afternoon and after dinner went around to White's. The club was almost deserted, but Dacre was pleased to see Robert

75

Stewart, Viscount Castlereagh, and Irish Chief Secretary, in the card room. Castlereagh ruthlessly deserted his game and came to meet Dacre as soon as he saw the Duke's bright head in the doorway.

"I'm delighted to see you, Castlereagh," Dacre said. "I had hardly hoped you would be able to get away."

"For something as important as this, Your Grace, I made it a point to get away," the young man answered. "I cannot exaggerate to you how important I feel this issue of allowing Catholics to sit in Parliament is for Ireland." The two men moved to a deserted corner of the room and sat down. Castlereagh rubbed an agitated hand across his face and said, "I virtually promised the Catholic Committee that Emancipation would follow the Union, Your Grace. You know that without the support of the Catholics the Act of Union never would have been carried in Ireland. We owe them something."

Dacre poured a glass of wine for Castlereagh and one for himself. "In good conscience," he said, "we owe Ireland justice. But since conscience is rarely a motive that sets the wheels of government turning, I might point out that our own political stability requires some kind of positive action in Ireland. If we allow the old internal struggles between Protestant and Catholic to continue, the only thing England will derive from the Union is increased expense. We would have been wiser to let the old Irish Parliament stand; after all, we controlled it quite effectively."

"Exactly." Castlereagh was surprised and pleased to find an English minister who understood the situation as he did. "In order for the Union, which is, I believe, in the best interests of both nations, in order, I say, for the Union to work, we must offer a demonstration of good faith to the bulk of the Irish people. Catholic Emancipation would be just such a demonstration."

"I am glad to hear you agree with me," Dacre said, and rose to his impressive height. "I have an appointment to meet with Pitt, Henry Dundas the War Secretary and Lord Grenville the Foreign Secretary tomorrow at two. Can you be there?"

"Where?"

"Downing Street."

"Yes."

"Good. I'll pick you up on my way."

Soon after, Dacre left White's and moved on to Brooks's, where he found his oldest friend, George Mowbray. Mowbray and Dacre had been at school, then at Cambridge together and, while Mowbray was not involved in government himself, he had followed his friend's career with great interest. Now, seeing Dacre's tall figure in the doorway, he called to him.

"How are you, George?" Dacre leisurely crossed the room. "And what are you doing in London in this heat?"

"Had to see my tailor, Charles. I go back to Bath tomorrow. Now, what's all this about your having married Christina MacCarthy? Is it true?"

Dacre's long fingers were busy with the decanter that lay on the table before Mowbray. "Yes, it's true," he answered briefly.

Mowbray looked at the polished head and flawless dress of his friend, then shook his head hopelessly. "I'll never understand you, Charles. You could have your pick of the marriage mart. There isn't a girl in London who wouldn't cheerfully sell her soul to be the Duchess of Dacre. And the title isn't all they're interested in, either. But what do you go and do? Marry an Irish rebel." Mowbray drained his glass and shook his head mournfully. "I'll never understand you, Charles," he repeated.

Dacre looked at his old friend; Mowbray's light brown hair was disordered, and he had loosened his cravat because of the heat. But his blue eyes were shrewd enough as they regarded the Duke. Suddenly, Dacre smiled. "Wait until you meet Christina, George. You'll understand immediately."

Mowbray cocked an eyebrow. "Like that, eh? But is she going to give up all this rabble-rousing, Charles?"

Dacre looked into the sympathetic eyes of his friend and sighed. "I hope so, George. I'm in town to see if we can get Pitt moving on Catholic Emancipation. If Parliament will only institute some much-needed reforms, Ireland—and Christina—will be satisfied."

Mowbray lifted his glass. "If any man can get that accomplished, Charles, you can. But what of the King? He's always been dead-set against Emancipation."

"If the Cabinet makes a unanimous recommendation to him, and Pitt uses all of his influence, he'll come around."

"For your sake, old friend, I hope so." Mowbray flourished his raised glass. "A toast! To the new Duchess of Dacre."

Dacre smiled. "Thank you, George," and they both raised their glasses to their lips.

Chapter Eight

"Put off that mask of burning gold
With emerald eyes."

—William Butler Yeats

Dacre spent the next morning at Westminster, talking to various members in the Lobby and over lunch. There was bitter division about the war. Most members agreed that Napoleon's defeat of Austria had given Britain her last chance for an honorable, negotiated peace. But whether she should take that chance or not was another issue.

The Duke picked up Lord Castlereagh at his hotel at one-forty-five and they had presented themselves in Downing Street by two o'clock. Mr. Dundas and Lord Grenville were already there.

No one had seen Dacre since his marriage, and the eyes trained on his arrogant, sunburned face were curious and penetrating. But the bronze mask of Dacre's control gave little away, and in all the following discussion his detached, objective, and lucid tone gave no indication of any personal interest in the subject under debate.

He opened the meeting by referring to Castlereagh. "I asked Lord Castlereagh to join us as he is one of the chief architects of the Union of Great Britain and Ireland and it is that Union I wish to speak of today. I asked Mr. Pitt to have both the War Secretary and the Foreign Secretary present also, as the Irish situation bears directly on our foreign affairs."

Dundas and Grenville looked at each other then back at Dacre. The Duke had acquired an impressive reputation during his five years in the Lords as a political intelligence of the highest caliber. If he were planning to take up the cudgels for Ireland, he would be well prepared to justify his decision. The rest of the room settled back to hear what he had to say.

His voice deep and steady, the clipped tones more than usually authoritative, Dacre opened his argument. "In a few months we will have seated at Westminster the first Parliament of the United Kingdom of Great Britain and Ireland. But, gentlemen, what will have really changed in the relations between these two countries? At present, the state of Ireland is as it has been for over six hundred years, a source of grave anxiety to England. For centuries we have tried to subdue this island to the west. We have conquered her not once, but many times. Nothing has served either to subdue or to reconcile her. What we have in Ireland today is what we have had for centuries: a hostile, lawless, oppressed, and poverty-stricken nation lying only a day's sail from Britain's coast. For centuries she has provided a refuge for enemy agents, a hatching ground for enemy plots, and—if the French landing at Bantry Bay had been successful—a launching point for enemy troops."

Dundas and Grenville leaned forward in their chairs, their eyes intent on Dacre. His green gaze, detached and passionless, looked back at them. The deep, steady voice continued.

"Now, gentlemen, how is the Act of Union we have just passed going to alter this situation? The government of Ireland is presently a military occupation, pure and simple, and the garrison of Ireland has sorely depleted us of troops needed elsewhere. Mr. Dundas will agree to that, I believe."

Tensely, Henry Dundas nodded his head.

Dacre looked at the three men facing him, briefly assessing their reactions, then continued. "We have at present in Ireland an alien, landlord, and Protestant garrison living in the midst of a native, Catholic, hostile peasantry. We have successfully contained all of the efforts of that peasantry to rebel and I believe we can continue to maintain our authority, but"—and here he looked directly at Dundas—"the cost of maintaining order requires an extensive military occupation. Can we afford this, gentlemen?"

"No." It was Lord Grenville who spoke. "We cannot. Not if we are going to continue the war with France."

"Even if the French war is safely concluded," Pitt was speaking now, "we still need to make some kind of peace with Ireland. Otherwise we will be committing British troops there, in ever-increasing numbers, for generations to come."

"Precisely, Mr. Pitt." Castlereagh spoke with dark intensity. "What His Grace has said about the state of Ireland is true. We instituted the Union to alleviate the hostility that now exists between the two kingdoms. If we wish to avoid governing Ireland on a garrison principle, if we wish Ireland to prove a resource rather than a burden, then an effort must be made to govern it through the public mind."

"And how can we do that, Lord Castlereagh?" the speaker was Henry Dundas.

"The first thing to do is to allow Catholics to sit in Parliament."

There was a moment's silence, then Dacre spoke softly. "How do you govern Ireland? Not by love, but by fear. Not by the confidence of the people in the laws and the constitution but by means of armed men and entrenched camps. Is that how it is to be, gentlemen?"

Pitt looked exhausted as he turned to Dundas and Grenville. "I have been in favor of Catholic Emancipation for some time," he said slowly, "but I have not been sure of the sentiments of the Cabinet."

Dundas looked at Dacre. "Will Catholic Emancipation keep Ireland quiet, Your Grace?"

"I don't know for how long," Dacre said frankly. "I do know that if we do not make a genuine effort to extend the benefits of the English constitution to the masses of the Irish people, we must be prepared to garrison Ireland indefinitely."

"We cannot afford that," repeated Lord Grenville. "I will do what I can to persuade the Cabinet to agree to an Emancipation bill."

"So will I," said Henry Dundas.

Pitt's head was throbbing as he stared at Dacre. He was the only one present who realized the magnitude of what Dacre had managed to bring off and for a moment his tired eyes looked enviously at the strong, bronzed face of his Home Secretary. Then he nodded. "Very well. After the recess, I shall call the Cabinet together to discuss the issue of Catholic Emancipation."

The future of Ireland's Union with Great Britain was on the minds of people other than the British

Cabinet. Dacre had been in London three weeks when Liam Emmet paid a visit to Christina at Strands.

The weeks had made quite a change in her appearance. Her face and figure had filled out to her normal healthy slenderness. Her skin was gold from the sun, her fair hair lighter than ever. Every waking moment she spent outdoors. After months of captivity, she could not get enough of it. As her strength came back, she began to exercise more vigorously. The countryside became accustomed to the sight of the new Duchess galloping her horse along the lake and up narrow mountain paths. Yet all the while her body gained in strength, a battle was being waged in the deep recesses of her conscious mind.

Dacre's leaving brought the first stirrings, but Christina, concentrating on her physical recovery, denied its existence. By dint of strenuous exercise, which brought healthy sleep, she managed to keep the unwanted question at the back of her mind. Liam's arrival forced it out into the open.

He was waiting for her one morning on the path by Lake Grasmere. She pulled up her horse in deep surprise, then dismounted. Her clear gray eyes looked at him soberly. "Liam," she said.

His brown gaze took her in. "You look well, MacCarthy More," he said deliberately.

Faint color rose in the golden glow of her cheeks. "Yes," she said simply. "I am very well, now." She turned and began to walk down the path. "Come, we can talk here." She led the way to a small clearing and sat on one of the wide rocks that circled it. "Why have you come?"

A tremor crossed Liam's young face. "To find out, of course," he said passionately. "Christina, why did you do it? Why did you marry him?"

And there it was, out in the open, square before her

83

waking mind. She circled around it. "To save my life, of course."

"I don't believe it," he said flatly. "You had only to eat to save your life. You didn't need to marry."

"But I couldn't get my freedom."

"You could have gotten your freedom the same way my brother and the rest of the United Irishmen did. You had simply to accept exile. You didn't need to marry the Duke of Dacre!" Anger and reproach trembled in his young voice.

Christina culled all her resources and spoke collectedly. "Liam, one has a different view of things from an English prison. My one desire in life is now, as it has always been, to alleviate the suffering of the Irish people. When I began to fast, it seemed to me that the only part left to me was to be a symbol. A symbol of resistance. But then the Duke offered me another way, and that seemed to me to be more effective."

"And what way is that?"

She spoke slowly. "The Duke believes in this Union. I don't. Ultimately, I think, Ireland will insist on her independence; but this I hope can come about peacefully. In the meantime, the Union offers us a number of advantages."

"Such as?"

"To alter the economic situation of Ireland requires a far-reaching change in the constitution, the admission of Catholics to Parliament, and the conferring of real representation to the people. The Irish Parliament would never have enacted these reforms. The Duke of Dacre has promised me to have these essential reforms enacted by the United Parliament."

Liam was on his feet. "And you believe him?"

Her eyes were steady. "Yes, Liam. I do believe him."

"You can't trust him!" he flung at her. "You can't trust any Englishman. You, more than anyone else, know that! He is a Sassenach, Christina. What does

84

he care about Ireland?" He came closer to her. "He wanted you, and so he said what you wanted to hear. But he won't keep his word."

"Stop it!" She jumped to her feet, her breath coming fast as though she had been running. "There comes a time, Liam, when you have to trust somebody. There is no hope for Ireland in open rebellion. We tried that and we failed. Now we have a British minister who has promised to try for constitutional reforms. He can only try. He is not Parliament. But he has a great deal of power, and he will use it for us. He offers the only hope I can see."

Liam walked to the edge of the clearing. "And that is why you married him?"

The pause was infinitesimal before she answered, "Yes, that is why I married him."

His voice was choked with emotion. "I hope, for all our sakes, he is faithful to his promise. But no matter what happens, remember that in Ireland you will find nothing but love."

Her smile only increased the ache in his heart. "Thank you, Liam. It is good to hear that."

Later that evening she stood by the window of her bedroom looking at the moon, the question raised by Liam written as brightly on her mind. The sound of her own voice echoed in her ears. "You are English and I am Irish. That is a gulf we could never bridge." And Liam's, "He is a Sassenach. What does he care about Ireland?" A whole tight and tangled web of reason and emotion struggled in the shadows of Christina's mind. She pressed her fingers on the sill and defied it for ninety seconds; then, as she was about to turn from the window, there came the sound of horses' hooves on the still night air. As she watched the drive, Dacre's phaeton came into sight. The moon illuminated the brightness of his hair as he stopped

85

the open carriage before the great door of Strands. He jumped down from the high seat, strong and lithe as a giant cat, turned the reins over to a servant, and began to walk toward the house.

Suddenly, graphic and revealing, the truth she had been hiding from for so long was brought home to Christina. She had lied to Liam. She had married Charles Standish for one reason only: out of all the wide and myriad world, he was the man for her. She had known it since that night in Kildare when he kissed her, but the implications had been too frightening to be acknowledged. The whole history of her country stood between them. But now, as she saw the front door close behind him, that didn't seem to matter.

Chapter Nine

I have never known love but as a kiss
In the mid-battle, and a difficult truce
Of oil and water, candles and dark night,
Hillside and hollow, the hot-footed sun
And the cold, sliding, slipper-footed moon—
A brief forgiveness between opposites....
—William Butler Yeats

Dacre had stayed in London until Parliament recessed at the end of July. He was busy; a financial
crisis kept him working late every night. With a major
effort of will, he forced himself to concentrate on business and suppress all thoughts of Christina. He was
not successful, but he managed.

Two days before he left for Cumberland he received
a visit from his Aunt Augusta. This in itself was startling, as she always spent the summers at Worthing.
But Lady Brinton had a severe sense of duty and,

hearing that her nephew was in town, had made the trip in the stifling heat expressly to see him.

When his butler announced her, Dacre knew immediately why she had come. She was his father's only surviving sister and, in Aunt Augusta's view, the House of Standish was of infinitely more note than the House of Hanover. Since his father's death, Dacre had been subjected to many orations about his duty as Head of the Family. Chief among them had been what his aunt regarded as his sacred duty to marry and beget more Standishes to carry on his illustrious line. Dacre had no doubt that it was his marriage that had brought his aunt post-haste to London. But he doubted also that she had come to congratulate him.

His expression, as his aunt was ushered into the room, was impeccably courteous. "Aunt Augusta," he said with lethal charm, as he went to kiss her cheek, "what a surprise. One had thought you to be at Worthing, doing whatever it is one does there."

Lady Brinton gripped her reticule more tightly. She made a rapid reassessment of the situation and decided to tread warily. There was no doing anything with Charles when he had that expression on his face. "I came about the notice in the paper," she said. "The one that announced your marriage to Christina MacCarthy."

"Yes?" his voice was pleasant.

"Is it true?"

"I sent it to the paper. It is true, as I imagine you know by now."

"Charles, how could you!" Caution was abandoned as Lady Brinton favored him with a thorough account of her opinion of his actions, responsibilities, and lack of family feeling. "If you expect me, or anyone else in society, to receive you, you must mistake the matter," she concluded. "A woman like that, a traitor, a prisoner, a murderer..." She stopped at the expression at Dacre's face.

There was a catastrophic silence. Then Dacre, speaking very softly, said, "You will receive Christina as the Duchess of Dacre, Aunt."

"I will not!" she answered angrily.

He waited a moment, then said in the same curious voice he had used all along, "If you do not, Aunt Augusta, you will irrevocably sever any relationship between us. I shall deny you and repudiate your family. In my eyes, the Standish family will cease to exist."

"Charles!" she cried out in protest.

He took a step nearer, and now she could see the anger in his eyes. "I shall, with difficulty, forget the words you just spoke about my wife. Or, I will forget you. Which shall it be, Aunt Augusta?"

She looked at the unyielding rock of his face, and her lips trembled. "I beg your pardon, Charles," she said, a quaver in her voice. "I shall be," she swallowed, "pleased to meet the new Duchess."

"Splendid." The rare warmth of his smile was her reward. "Will you stay to dinner?"

"Yes, thank you," she said. And they spent the evening speaking of other things.

Dacre thought briefly of this meeting as he drove homeward. Poor Aunt Augusta, so ruthlessly sacrificed to Christina's superior need. But her adjustment to the life of the Duchess of Dacre was going to be difficult enough without having social ostracism to cope with.

The problem of Christina, so resolutely ignored these past weeks, occupied him exclusively for the remainder of his journey north. How was she? Had that uncharacteristic and frightening apathy gone? How would she feel about his return?

Charles Standish had some grasp of the difficulties

that lay ahead of him in this marriage. He had not just married a woman, he had married a cause. He was prepared, for her sake and for the sake of justice, to wage battle for that cause. If they were both working together for the same thing, he reasoned, the divisions between them would heal. The fear that she would eventually ask far more of him than he was prepared to give, he kept securely fastened below the borders of his conscious mind.

When he reached Kendal, he decided to have dinner and push on to Strands. It was eleven o'clock at night when he reached home and, on being told the Duchess had retired, he went upstairs and along the picture-hung hallway to her room. He knocked gently and heard her voice call "Come in."

She was standing by the window, which was open to let in the cool air and the moonlight. She wore a silk robe over a nightgown trimmed with delicate embroidery. The moonlight gave her an otherworldly look and she didn't move as he came in and closed the door behind him.

"I just got home," he said unnecessarily. "I thought I'd look in on you to see how you were doing."

"I'm much better, thank you," she said in a strange voice.

"Things went very well in London. I believe we have a good chance of getting Cabinet support for an Emancipation Bill." He came further into the room so that the moonlight caught him in its brightness. As she looked at his strong, beautiful face, she knew that any chance of keeping their relationship on a purely pragmatic basis was impossible. Slowly, with the motions of a sleepwalker, she came to where he stood and looked up at him.

His green eyes searched her face, relieved to see it restored to the healthy glow that had been there at their first meeting. But he looked too at the altered expression in her eyes as her smoky gaze met his. Christina felt herself swept by an unfamiliar yet compelling emotion and her wide, gray eyes were dark with it. She looked up at him and said gravely, "I am afraid," for her life had been suddenly channeled into new and strange ways, and she had lost her bearings.

"There is no need," he said softly. "Little eagle, I have loved you since first I saw you. I would give my life before I hurt you." A quiver passed over her face and he said, a harsher note in his voice, "You are my wife, Christina, but I will make no claims on you." With great difficulty, he stepped back from her. "None," he said again, "except what you want to give."

A small smile hovered around the corners of her mouth. "Do you really mean that, Charles?"

"Yes, I do. But I give you fair warning, Christina, if you come any closer I am going to take you, like it or not. I couldn't stop myself."

The gravity of her face was broken by a real smile as she stepped toward him, her arms held out. His hands reached out to encircle her and she rested her palms on either side of his face. "Charles," her voice was soft as a caress. He bent his head and, as a parched man seeks water, sought her mouth. At the touch of his lips the unfamiliar emotion within her swelled into a torrent. She clung to him, her body taut and trembling under his mouth and his hands. He lifted her in his arms and carried her to the bed.

This time there was no one to interrupt. Christina's body throbbed with an almost unbearable tension, and she reached out to Dacre for a release she didn't understand. All she knew was that if he left her now, she would shatter into a million pieces. Blindly, trustingly, she obeyed his guidance. Then a sudden sharp pain flashed through her and instinctively she tried to pull away from him. But he held her close, his voice in her ear, and the pain was mixed with something else, a

91

spreading flood of delight which shook her body and took her breath.

She lay against the coolness of the sheets and looked at his face above her, its strong planes revealed by the moonlight. Gently she raised a hand and traced the contour of his lips. Nothing else matters, she thought. Only Charles. He said something in a voice ·even deeper than usual and a smile curved her lips. Only the moon looked on, shining through the open window, catching gleams from the two fair heads, one gold and one silver, so close together in the big bed.

The sun-dappled August weeks slipped by, a haven out of time for Christina and for Dacre. They spent their days outdoors, as their bleached hair and tanned skin betrayed. At night they came together in the big bed slept in by so many generations of Standishes, and the love and passion that they found were shattering in their intensity. For Christina, the powerful physical presence of Dacre blurred the sharp edges of her national outrage and lit her spirit with joy. Dacre found himself constantly amazed by the depth of desire she provoked in him and the peace she alone could give him. She knew nothing of love but what he had taught her and, knowing that, she knew everything.

"I'm happy," she told him with surprise one cloudy afternoon as they made their way back from a fishing expedition on the lake. "It's been so long since I could say that. Years, it seems."

He looked at her strong, slender figure, walking so straightly beside him. "I intend to make happiness a staple of your diet from now on," he told her. "I'll administer it in regular daily doses, like an apothecary."

Her flashing smile broke out, white in the golden tan of her face. "Ah, therein the physician doth administer to himself."

His green eyes glinted. "Are you accusing me of self-interest?"

"'He who helps a friend gives glory to himself as well,'" she quoted.

He laughed, and the first drops of rain touched their faces. Their pace quickened. "In a way," he said, "such happiness is frightening. For someone like myself, for whom living has always been an abstract game played with one's brain, this kind of emotional investment in someone else is dreadfully upsetting."

She stopped suddenly and turned to face him, the rain falling unregarded on her upturned face. His whole life lay bare before her in that one sentence. "Why?" she said. "You have a great capacity for love. I, of all people, know that."

He reached out and touched her wet cheek. "I have never loved anyone but you. You are my one bond to the world. You said you were afraid." His voice was perfectly sober. "So am I."

She shook her head in denial, and reached up to cover his lips with her hand. "Don't talk to me of fear. Talk of love." They clung together, their wet clothes hardly concealing their bodies from each other. In her cool rain-washed lips, Dacre read the fear she was trying to deny. "Nothing can come between us," she whispered fiercely. "Nothing!"

His arms tightened around her urgently. "Let's go home," he said. Her rain-darkened head nodded in reply.

Inevitably the subject of Ireland arose. Dacre's own vast holdings brought it up at first. He owned estates in Derbyshire, Yorkshire, Lancashire, Lincolnshire, Sussex, Middlesex, and Scotland as well as Strands, and he personally went over all the accounts of his properties and all important questions with his estate agents. Christina's experience of landlords had not prepared her for the hard work and time that Dacre put into the supervision of his holdings. In addition, the tenants at Strands obviously regarded the Duke with affection as well as respect. This aspect of Dacre was a revelation to her, and she questioned him about it.

"I am not a paragon, by any means," he told her with a hint of amusement. "The answer lies, I think, in the land system. Most of my tenants have been on their farms for generations. They pay me a reasonable rent and for my part I see that the farm is adequately equipped. Buildings, drainage works, and so forth, are constructed at my expense. The benefits accrue to both tenant and landlord. There is a community of interest between us, mutually recognized and respected."

"You live on your lands," she said slowly. "That also is a difference. The absentee landlord is one of Ireland's biggest plagues."

"I realize that. I do not say that the English aristocracy is the best governing body in the world, but it is, at least, in touch with the central and serious current of life in the nation. That comes from passing at least half the year in the country. It is not a protected existence."

For the first time in weeks a hint of bitterness crept into her voice. "The Irish aristocracy spend a few weeks a year, at most, on their lands. There is no relationship at all between landowner and tenant; no common community of interest. What is more, a tenant has no security of tenure. A family may be, and often is, evicted without notice. The farms are let barren, all equipment to be supplied by the tenant. Any improvement the tenant may make to his holding becomes, when his lease expires or is terminated, the property of the landlord. Without compensation to the tenant."

They were having a glass of wine in the drawing room before going up to change for dinner. Dacre looked at the glowing amber of his glass, then at his wife. "I know, little eagle," he said gently. "We will do something about it."

She put down her glass. "What, Charles?" she asked.

His voice altered to a tone both calm and academic. "First, we will bring about a bill for Catholic Emancipation. Once Catholics can sit in Parliament, we will have to shift our emphasis from Westminster to Ireland." There was a pause, as he looked challengingly into her wide gray eyes. "Will the Irish peasantry stand up to their landlords and vote for committed Catholic candidates?"

The corners of her mouth folded with pressure. "You mean to ask them to defy the people who hold the power of life and death over them, who for generations have bought and sold their votes as if they were cattle?"

"No nation has freedom today that has not been willing to fight for it. Will they?"

Slowly her pale head nodded. "Yes, Charles. If properly organized, I believe they will."

He leaned forward and spoke intently. "Even a small Irish party, Christina, could disrupt the business of Parliament. If Ireland can send a committed group of members to Westminster, then, by a shrewd combination of skill and tenacity, we should be able to deal on equal terms with—and eventually, perhaps, hold the balance between—the two major English parties. That is the way to win land reform: through constitutional agitation, not out on the hillside."

She sat perfectly still, her face grave in the softening light. "The path you point to, Charles, requires consummate political ability. There is no man in Ireland who has had the opportunity to acquire such skill. Who will lead us?"

"I will," he said.

"As a Tory minister?"

Dacre's face held all of its usual serene arrogance. "Until the Emancipation Bill is passed, at any rate. After that, we shall see." He smiled at her. "Give us a little credit for common sense, Christina. Ireland is the only country in the civilized world where the entire agricultural population can be evicted by the mere whim of the landlord. Hardly a stable situation. And England, especially now that she is engaged in war, wants, above all things, stability in Ireland. That is our ultimate weapon, after all. It is in England's self-interest to placate Ireland. We will win, I think."

There was a pause, then she said urgently, "We must, Charles. We must."

On September 5, Dacre returned home in the late afternoon having spent the day with his lawyer in Kendal. When he asked for Christina, his major domo replied, his face as rigid as stone, "Her Grace is in the garden, Your Grace. A man," he paused, then continued, the disapproving note more noticeable, "an Irishman, called to see her. They have been out there for about two hours."

Dacre's hard green eyes raked Yeadon's face. "What was his name?"

"Murdoch Lynch, Your Grace."

Dacre nodded and walked through the house to the morning room, which had French doors leading out to the garden. He stood for a moment in the doorway, unobserved. They were standing at the farthest end of the garden, facing each other. Dacre could see the tension in Christina's figure from as far away as the doorway. Then the man put both hands on her shoulders and said something intensely. She answered and

96

he slid an arm around her and hugged her. Dacre was unprepared for the flash of primitive jealousy that went through him. After what they had known together, he wasn't prepared to surrender any part of Christina. And Murdoch Lynch, imprisoned rebel and friend of Niall MacCarthy, recently pardoned by Cornwallis, Murdoch Lynch represented the dark third in his marriage. He represented Ireland. His tanned face a bronze mask, Dacre walked forward to greet his wife and her visitor.

The first thing Murdoch Lynch had done when he was so surprisingly released from Kilmainham Gaol was to go to see Christina MacCarthy. He had known her since she was a child of seven and he at twenty-three a devoted admirer of her father. Through the Earl of Clancarthy, Murdoch became involved with the United Irishmen movement. He was arrested three days after Clancarthy was killed and had been in jail ever since. Cornwallis's surprise pardon, designed to conciliate, had not been politic in Murdoch's case. His life was devoted to his country. When people asked him why he hadn't married, he often answered that he was already married to Ireland. Only Murdoch knew that whatever heart he had left to spare had been irrevocably given to a seven-year-old child who had turned into the most beautiful woman in the world.

He had talked to Liam Emmet, but felt he needed to see Christina for himself in order to decide on further action. Murdoch had no intention of resting from his labors, but Christina was the single most important figure in Irish Catholic politics, and nothing could be planned until he spoke with her.

He was finding the interview difficult. The Christina who met him was not the Christina he knew. She had always reminded him of a snow princess, perfect as the moon and as unattainable; to be worshiped, not to be touched.

From the first minutes of their conversation he had been aware that the snow princess was no more. There was a quality about her that she had not had before; the aura of a woman whose senses have been awakened. He watched her closely as they walked about the garden. Her features were the same; it was something in her eyes, he thought, and in the timbre of her voice. Her austere beauty was underlit by an unconscious sensuousness and the effect was dizzying. Murdoch had a very difficult time trying to concentrate on her words. He found himself intensely curious to meet the Duke of Dacre, the man who had changed his snow maiden into the woman who stood beside him now.

His curiosity was shortly to be satisfied. "I'll have to discuss this with Liam and John Farrell, Christina," he said. "I am creating a new executive board and we will be meeting shortly to discuss strategy. But they will want to know just what Dacre is promising. How far is he willing to go in the area of reform?"

Christina looked into the finely-drawn face of the man facing her. Prison had exaggerated that look of fragility he had always had, but the fire of his spirit was evident in the brilliance of his eyes. "Murdoch," she said wearily, "the only alternative to Charles is the hillside again. You and I and Liam and John Farrell know only too well the futility of that."

He looked into her lovely, troubled face and felt again the bitter anger he had lived with during her imprisonment and fast. He hugged her briefly, rejoicing in the feel of her, warm and living, against him. "I know, Christina," he said. "We will discuss it." He looked up then and saw, crossing the lawn toward him, Charles Standish, Duke of Dacre.

Christina's clear gray eyes were dark with trouble

as she introduced the two men. The Duke was impeccably courteous, his voice easy and pleasant as he spoke to the Irishman. But it was clear to Murdoch, beyond any shadow of a doubt, that the Duke of Dacre did not want him here.

"Murdoch is reorganizing an executive board to direct Irish affairs, Charles," Christina said. "The leaders of the United Irishmen are all in exile," she paused, "or dead," she added flatly, and both men immediately thought of Niall MacCarthy. "But there are a few people who managed to escape the English net, and Murdoch is organizing them. We will need support in Ireland for a constitutional battle at Westminster. Murdoch will see that we get it."

Murdoch's intense blue eyes were on Dacre's face. "Christina's recommendation will go a long way toward influencing the Irish, Your Grace. But they will want to know, specifically, what you mean when you talk about land reform."

Dacre's voice was expressionless as he answered the Irishman. "My wife and I will be coming to Ireland in a month or so. At that time I will present my program to your board for their consideration."

Murdoch's eyes went immediately to Christina. There was a tense silence, then Christina said slowly, "Charles can't work in a vacuum, Murdoch. If you are going to trust him at all, you will have to trust him all the way. He will have to meet them."

Some of the tenseness went out of Murdoch's face and he nodded. "All right." He held out his hand to Dacre. "We will see you in a month, Your Grace." He turned to say good-bye to Christina.

"Wait," she said. "I'll ride with you as far as Grasmere. Just let me get my jacket." She disappeared into the house, leaving the two men alone.

A few clouds had moved in, breaking the clear blue of the sky and casting shadows on the garden where they stood. There was between them the inevitable hostility that arises between men who love the same woman and the silence was static with the unspoken. Then Murdoch said bluntly, "Are you doing this for Christina, Duke?"

Dacre was equally blunt. "Yes."

Murdoch's narrow face was bleak. "When I heard about her fast, I wanted to tear the world apart. You saved her life and for that I am grateful." He looked at the arrogant, sunburned face of Christina's husband and then said soberly, "But I know Christina, Duke, and she didn't agree to give up her fast just to marry you. You saved her for Ireland, as well as for yourself. Never forget that."

Dacre's voice was brittle with hard-controlled temper as he answered. "I will lead your fight for Catholic Emancipation and for land reform, Mr. Lynch. And we will base our appeals on the English constitution. Let me make myself perfectly clear: I do not want my wife involved with any further rebellious schemes."

The hostility was open now, and unmistakable. "So long as there is hunger and destitution in Ireland, Your Grace, there will be rebellion. And if you think Christina will turn her back on her people, you are greatly mistaken." Then they heard Christina's step and turned to watch her as she came up to them, clear and proud and beautiful. In a few minutes she and Murdoch were mounted and riding side by side down the narrow drive toward Grasmere. Dacre stood watching them, his face like granite.

Christina was gone for several hours, coming home just in time to change for dinner. She was quieter than usual and excused herself immediately after the last course, saying she was tired. Dacre sat for a long time over his wine, then went upstairs himself to their bedroom.

The room was dark and Christina stood at the opened windows looking out on the night. It had begun to rain. She pulled her robe closely about her and said, "It's September. The summer's over. You can feel it in the chill of the rain."

Dacre closed the door behind him and spoke very gently. "What is wrong, little eagle?"

She continued to stare out the window. "Seeing Murdoch, I guess. He reminded me of my father."

And there between them for the first time since their marriage was the strain between conqueror and conquered, between the man who had lost nothing and the girl who had had her father shot down, her land plundered, her freedom taken. His voice was carefully neutral. "Christina, there is nothing to be gained by dwelling on past injuries. Your father would be the first one to urge you to look to the future."

"The future is built on the past," she answered him.

"Then let us use the future to redress the grievances of the past. Do not make a division between us where there is none."

Her eyes, bottomless gray pools in her strained face, searched his. "Murdoch asked me the one question I have been avoiding having to face. He asked what I would do if you were unsuccessful with Parliament."

"That is the bridge I hope never to have to cross," he said harshly. "God, Christina, you are questioning my good faith?"

"No!" she said quickly. "Of course not, Charles."

"Then let's leave it," he said. He moved to the window and closed it, then turned to her. "You're freezing." He picked her up and carried her over to the bed. "Nothing is more important than this," he murmured as his mouth came down on hers.

101

Her response was instant, as she reached up to pull him down beside her. But deep in the back of her mind, before his kisses blotted out all thought, was a faint protest: What about my country?

Chapter Ten

> Love is all
> Unsatisfied
> That cannot take the whole
> Body and soul.
>
> —William Butler Yeats

Murdoch Lynch's visit did indeed seem to signal the end of summer. The weather turned misty and cold, with a chill wind that whipped color into the faces of those who stepped outdoors. Christina awoke very early on the morning they were to leave for London. The light outside the window was gray and the air in the bedroom frigid. She snuggled down under the quilt, close to the warmth of Dacre. He slept on his side with his face turned away from her. He was a quiet sleeper who was easily awakened, so she lay still next to him, her eyes on the smoothly muscled width of his bare back. Out of the tangled mesh of emotions in her heart, came a prayer. "Dear God," she prayed silently, "give us success." The prospect of London loomed before her like an ogre in a fairytale. The Cabinet would meet and decide whether or not to press for Catholic Emancipation. If they decided not to?

Murdoch's visit had brought that question out into the open and now it preyed on Christina's mind. If he failed, what would she do? "You are English and I am Irish. That is a gulf we could never bridge." Her head moved sharply on the pillow, in denial. Disturbed by her sudden motion, he woke and turning, raised himself on one elbow to look at her, alert as he always was on first awakening. She reached a hand up and traced the line of his jaw and down the strong column of neck and chest. His short gold hair was tousled as a small boy's.

"What is it?" he asked, his voice deep and even.

"I love you," she answered.

Her silver hair streamed on the pillow, framing her face and eyes, dark with trouble and with something else. He reached out and undid the small pearl buttons of her thin nightgown and with his mouth found the smooth, perfect roundness of her small breasts. The familiar, welcome fire ran through her, as his hands slid up the length of her slender body.

"I love you, I love you," she repeated, a charm to keep them safe and warm against the cold and uncertainty of the mist outside.

They left for London and on September 25, under the combined pressure of Dacre, Castlereagh, and Cornwallis, Pitt wrote to Lord Chancellor Loughborough, who was in attendance upon the King at Weymouth, asking for his presence at a Cabinet meeting to discuss the Catholic question.

The meeting, as Dacre reported to Christina, was stormy. Pitt proposed to abolish the oaths recognizing the supremacy of the Church of England and abjuring the Church of Rome which each newly-elected member of Parliament had to swear. In their place, he proposed a mere oath of allegiance.

"Loughborough is a life-long bigot," Dacre told Christina. "He did not like it at all. Neither did Portland or Westmoreland."

"Who was for it?"

"Pitt, of course. And Castlereagh and Cornwallis. Even Locke, who can hardly be accused of liberal tendencies was for it."

"What was said?" she asked tensely.

He settled himself more comfortably in his chair, his long legs in their gleaming boots stretched before him. "Cornwallis was splendid." His eyes narrowed with the effort of memory. "He told them that the ancient edifice of the Irish constitution was a monstrous assumption of injustice and inequities and since it was not possible to reform it he had always felt its destruction was a deed well done. But if those inequities and injustices were not redressed by the United Parliament of Great Britain and Ireland he would regret ever lifting a hand in the affair."

"I imagine that made a great impression," Christina said dryly.

He cocked an eyebrow. "Moral imperatives have never been the most forceful arguments when one is dealing with the Cabinet."

"So I gathered. What else happened?"

"Well, Castlereagh did a little better. He pointed out that where Catholic Emancipation under the Irish constitution would have allowed the large numbers of Irish Catholics to swamp the Protestants, in a Parliament for the whole British Isles the Catholics would always be in a small minority and therefore harmless."

"What a nice man," Christina spoke briskly. "I

imagine that kind of political cynicism was more effective?"

"It was. I added a few well-chosen words, and we ended up with Cabinet approval."

"A few well-chosen words," she murmured. "And what were they, Your Grace?"

He looked faintly amused. "Threats, my love. I made a very brief speech on the effectiveness of terrorist activities in Ireland, the remarkable cohesiveness the protests over your imprisonment had shown, and ended up by pointing out the dangers and expense of maintaining a large garrison in Ireland during a time of war. Dundas and Grenville leaped to my support, and the others followed suit."

Her face blazed with excitement. "What comes next, Charles?"

"Pitt will introduce the Bill to the House after the first of the year. The Commons will be no problem. It is the Lords we have to worry about." Her brows drew together and he smiled at her reassuringly. "I think we can do it, but there is where you can help, little eagle."

"How?"

"I think Parliament, and hence the London Social Season, will open early this year. We will be invited to parties, balls, routs, the opera, et cetera, et cetera."

"I'm afraid I don't quite understand how my socializing with English society is going to affect the government's vote on Catholic Emancipation, Charles."

"It will, because the people who sit at Westminster are the very people who go to those balls and parties. There are, I would say, about two hundred families who have been governing England for generations. Everyone knows or is related to everyone else. Make a favorable impression on the people you meet every day. Convince them that Ireland is anxious for reform, not for revolution. That is the way to win votes for Catholic Emancipation."

Christina's patrician nose rose a trifle. "I had no idea, Charles, that the great English Parliament was such a family club."

"Well, it is," he told her. "Don't be such a snob, Christina."

At that, she laughed. "I've fought for Ireland, I've been imprisoned for Ireland, I guess, Charles, I can even be fashionable for Ireland."

"Spoken like a true patriot," he applauded. "Do you dance?"

"I beg your pardon?"

"I asked if you danced," he repeated patiently.

"I shoot rather well."

"Excellent."

"And I'm one of the best horsemen in Ireland."

"I've noticed."

"I roll a pretty mean pair of dice."

"You do?" He was diverted. "I'll have to see for myself sometime."

"But," she said regretfully, "my dancing is rather rusty, I'm afraid."

"How rusty?"

"I believe my mother taught me some steps when I was nine."

"Ah."

"I suppose, in order to be fashionable in England, one must dance?"

"I would say so."

"Can you teach me?"

"If you'll teach me how to roll dice."

"It's a bargain," she said.

The next few weeks Dacre devoted to what Christina called her "education in frivolity." They shopped for clothes, and Christina had to bite her lip to keep from remonstrating about the sums Dacre expended. Dozens of daytime dresses and formal gowns were ordered as well as gloves and hats and pelisses and shoes and shawls. Christina had an innate love of beauty and could not help but be pleased by the beautiful fabrics; and the simple Grecian cuts then in style exactly suited her taste. But she felt guilty about the money.

Dacre laughed at her. "Think of it as money spent on ammunition," he told her.

She shook her head, elegantly coifed in a smooth chignon. "Was all that really necessary?"

"Yes. Besides," he turned to grin at her, "I like spending money on you."

Answering laughter warmed her face. "The money doesn't impress me. It's the sore toes from the dancing lessons that are the real proof of love."

He winced in memory. "You're doing beautifully now, my love. All we need to do at this point is engage a lady's maid to look after all this finery, and then we can leave for Ireland." Under the cover of shifting his reins, he observed her closely.

"Ireland," she said softly, her fine skin still flushed a little with laughter. There was a short silence as Christina contemplated the coming meeting between Dacre and the Irish leadership. The Irishmen were not at all like the men Dacre was used to dealing with at Westminster. Murdoch was the son of a lawyer, John Farrell was a farmer, and Liam's father had been a doctor. They were not great landowners and rulers; they were not of Dacre's class. They were talented, dedicated men whose sympathies were totally out of tune to everything generations of Standishes had stood for. Not for the first time Christina was conscious of great uneasiness about the coming meeting.

"They will like your reform plan," she said finally.

"It is what we wanted from the old Irish Parliament, and more."

"Our meeting must remain a strict secret, Christina. If word ever got back to Westminster, it would be the death of Emancipation. Lynch is quite sure there is no chance of an informer being present?"

"We learned our lesson in ninety-eight, Charles," her voice was bitter. "We are trusting no one whose loyalty has not been proven. I don't even know who will be there. Murdoch won't trust the mails. We will have to wait until we get to Dublin. He will contact us then."

Dacre nodded curtly. "I don't like this secrecy, Christina, but it is necessary until the Emancipation Bill is passed. After that, all our activities will be perfectly constitutional and able to be conducted in public."

The curve of Christina's mouth was wry. "Secrecy and midnight meetings in strange places may be strange to you, Charles, but not as strange, I assure you, as daylight organization will be to us."

They arrived home to find that Lady Brinton had called. She was waiting for them in the drawing room, Dacre's butler informed them. She had been there forty-five minutes.

Dacre nodded to Foster and turned to Christina. "She must be curious, indeed, little eagle. We'll have to see her. Do you want to freshen up first?"

Christina laughed and shook her head. "It's an old rule in Ireland, Charles, never keep an aunt waiting."

"You don't have aunts like my Aunt Augusta," he said with amusement.

The smile still lingered on Christina's lips as they entered the drawing room. Lady Brinton turned at the sound of Dacre's voice and saw Christina framed in the doorway. She saw a tall, slender girl dressed in a fashionable tunic of burgundy velvet over a pure white muslin gown. Her pale hair was drawn back into an elegant chignon, her face softened only by the pearls in her ears. The fine-boned beauty of that face startled Lady Brinton, who looked immediately at her nephew. Dacre's face was grave, but his eyes held a glint of malice as he presented his wife to his aunt and settled back to watch the results.

Christina was splendid, he thought; charming, with just a hint of reserve in her manner. Lady Brinton as she recovered from the surprise Christina's beauty and elegance had given her, began to feel more cheerful about her nephew's wife. Her speech was excellent: cultured and accentless. She looked positively English with that silver hair; somehow, Lady Brinton had thought all the Irish were dark.

Dacre watched Christina from under his lashes as his aunt continued on in this vein. At first his wife looked surprised, then embarrassed for Lady Brinton, then—as she realized she was being condescended to—astonished. Lady Brinton was well-launched on her favorite topic, the sacredness of the great Standish family, when Christina finally found her voice. What she said to Lady Brinton was, Dacre told her later, a privilege to hear. She was definite, calm, polite, and devastating. Lady Brinton left in a turmoil of mixed emotions, having been reminded indirectly that while Christina's husband was addressed as Your Grace, her grandfather was Your Majesty.

Christina looked at Dacre indignantly as he returned from escorting his ruffled aunt to her carriage. "Really, Charles! She is the limit!"

He grinned. "She gets worse, as you get to know her better."

Some of the glitter left Christina's eye. "Impossible. Imagine, wondering how I learned to talk. How does anyone learn to talk?"

"Poor Aunt Augusta," he shook his head sorrowfully. "She just suffers from an excess of family pride. How was she to know she'd encountered an even bigger snob than herself?"

"What!" Christina was rigid with outrage.

"Be fair, little eagle. Aunt Augusta just assumed, not without cause, that anyone would be proud to marry a Standish. Becoming Duchess of Dacre meant nothing to you, not because you had not enough pride but because you had too much. You were already Christina MacCarthy; what was there to aim at beyond?"

"Don't be ridiculous." Her voice was severe. Then, as he merely cocked an eyebrow at her, she softened. "Being your wife means something to me."

"I'm glad to hear that. And now we'd better get dressed for dinner."

She accompanied him up the stairs, turning to remark as they reached the landing, "Your Aunt Augusta is nothing, Charles, to what you'll find in Ireland."

"What do you mean?"

"Your true Irishman genuinely feels that he is the most intelligent, witty, handsome, and beloved by God of all races on earth. There is only one thing that makes his conceit at all bearable."

"And what is that?"

She looked at him, the ghost of true delight in her eyes. "He's right," she said.

A minor domestic crisis intervened to delay their departure. The lady's maid had been duly acquired and the girl who had been acting as Christina's personal maid returned to her original duties. Her name was Jenny and she, as were so many of the Standish servants, was from Cumberland. The bags were packed and all in train to leave for Ireland when Dacre came into Christina's dressing room one morning to

111

be met by a very straight-backed Christina and a sobbing Jenny. In a moment the girl had run past him out into the hall and along the corridor, her hands to her face.

Dacre closed the door and turned to his wife. Her face was hard and bright; it took him a moment to realize that she was furious. "What has happened?" he asked.

She took a deep breath, forcing herself to relax. When she spoke, her voice was cool and clipped. "I have been concerned for some time about Jenny. I've seen quite a lot of her lately, and certain things are difficult to hide. Today I asked her directly, offering to help." As he still looked puzzled, she said briefly, "She is pregnant."

Dacre's eyes, clear and green as the sea, were steady on her face. "That isn't what upset you," he said.

Her mouth was taut. "I asked her who the father was. I thought perhaps it might be possible to arrange a marriage."

He was very still. "And what did she say?"

"She said you were responsible."

He had a sudden vision of Jenny, a black-haired north-country girl with red cheeks and luscious curves. He looked at his wife, delicate and strong as a wild creature, her wide, severe brow framed by the softly-drawn-back moonlight of her hair. His own voice was detached as he said, "And you want to know if she is telling the truth?"

She had walked to the window, but at that she swung around. "Charles!" Incredulity was in her voice. "Of course she isn't telling the truth." Her eyes blazed. "How dare she slander you like that? I was so angry I almost struck her." Scorn rang in her voice. "But all she could do was cry."

His voice was steady, but there was something in it that pierced the shell of her anger and focused all

112

her attention on him. "How can you be so sure?" he asked.

She crossed the room until she stood directly before him. "Because I know you."

His mouth twisted. "Do you take me for such a saint?"

Her gaze never faltered. "No. I have a very good idea of what you are. And you are not a man who would take advantage of an unprotected girl who is a member of your household."

He rested his cheek on the top of her shining hair. When he spoke his voice was very gentle. "'By hir the vertue of the starrs downe slide, In hir is vertues perfect image cast.'" He looked at her, his eyes very bright in his tan face. "I don't deserve you. But I have no intention of giving you up."

She reached up to briefly touch his cheek. "I hope not. But what are we going to do about Jenny?"

He frowned. "I don't know. God knows what made her blame me."

Christina looked from his strong slender hands to the beautiful, arrogant lines of his face. Her eyes suddenly sparkled with mischief. "Wishful-thinking, I expect," she said.

He looked startled, then, to her infinite delight, embarrassed. "Don't be ridiculous," he said shortly.

Christina straightened her shoulders. "Well, we can't have her going around telling everyone you are her seducer. I shall have to get to the bottom of it." He watched her march to the door. "If only she wouldn't cry so much!" she said disgustedly.

True to her word, Christina got Jenny to admit that she had been having an affair with one of the Duke's young grooms. She had feared to get him dismissed from his post. With great dispatch, the Duchess saw the two young people married and packed off to Strands where they could live in one of the estate

113

cottages. True to form, Jenny cried copiously through all the proceedings.

Finally, on October 15, the Duke and Duchess of Dacre departed for Ireland.

Chapter Eleven

"I am of Ireland,
  And the Holy Land of Ireland,
  And time runs on," cries she.
"Come out of charity,
  And dance with me in Ireland."
                    —William Butler Yeats

Christina's return to her native land was a notable event in the affairs of Ireland in 1800. She had left a prisoner and proclaimed enemy of the state; she returned as the Duchess of Dacre, wife of the Home Minister of the very state she had been imprisoned for opposing. Under the circumstances, the Protestant ministers and nobility hardly knew how to treat her. Christina maintained a regal calm throughout her entire visit that was matched by Dacre's distant courtesy and implacable reserve. The Irish Establishment found them distinctly unnerving.

But if the nobility did not know how to deal with Christina, clearly the masses did. Everywhere she went she was followed by large, enthusiastic crowds who cried her name and cheered her every gesture. Dacre was astonished. "The last time I escorted you through Dublin we came in at the dead of night for fear of the people's anger against you."

"Oh, there are many people in Dublin who have no love for me, Charles," she answered. "They are silenced at present, due to our marriage. But"—and here she turned to look at the crowd gathered around their carriage—"there are many more who follow me, as they followed my father. I am glad"—her voice was soft—"they do not think I have deserted them."

Dacre looked at the large, milling crowd of people and heard again the cries of "MacCarthy More" that had been in his ears since their arrival. "I hope their leaders are as ready to follow you as these are, little eagle," he said soberly.

She put her hand on his. "We'll soon know, Charles. We're to meet with Murdoch tomorrow. In Wicklow."

It was not exactly the midnight meeting Christina had once spoken of; in fact, it took place at nine in the morning in a small cottage in the Wicklow hills. Dacre and Christina had been in the saddle before six, slipping out of Mallon House by the back way. Liam Emmet met them on the outskirts of Dublin and took them the rest of the way.

It was a meeting of some significance, this first encounter between the English aristocrat and the Irish revolutionaries who had agreed to listen to his program. There were four men gathered around a rough-hewn table when Christina and Dacre entered with Liam. Murdoch, of course, more fragile looking than ever; John Farrell, a veteran of the uprising in Wexford, who had been released from Kilmainham with

Murdoch; Sean Molloy, who had been at Slea Castle with Christina; and—Christina's eyes widened slightly—Michael Walsh, whose ties to the Defenders, a secret society pledged to agrarian agitation, were well known to her.

Their welcome to Christina was emotional and genuine; with Dacre they were guarded. Christina introduced him all around, and they took seats around the rough oval table. Christina spoke first. "We asked Murdoch to call you together in order to present to you a plan of action for Ireland." Around the table the hardening of their attention was plain to see. She turned to her husband and said simply, "Charles?"

Dacre had no papers with him. Bareheaded and unsmiling, he glanced around and then spoke, pleasantly and without raising his voice. "Gentlemen, the English Cabinet has pledged itself to bring in Catholic Emancipation."

Murdoch's chair scraped as he moved abruptly. "Do you mean it, Dacre?"

"Yes. It will come up after the United Parliament convenes in January. The Commons will vote for it and I think we have a good chance of swinging the Lords as well."

"What of the King?" It was Liam Emmet's young voice.

Dacre looked at him, his green eyes level. "The King takes the advice of his Prime Minister. We must leave him to Pitt."

"This is all very well, Dacre." The speaker was Sean Molloy, the man who had fought with Christina. "But what is Emancipation going to do for Ireland? The Irish members will always be outnumbered in an English Parliament."

Dacre regarded the flaming red hair and restless eyes of Molloy. "Catholic Emancipation is only the first step, Mr. Molloy. What I am proposing is a total constitutional struggle, aimed at winning major land reform for Ireland."

"Are we to rely on the good will of Mr. Pitt and the Tories, then?" It was Murdoch's voice now.

"I would not depend upon any English political party. I should not advise you to depend upon any English political party. In this great issue, Ireland must stand alone." He paused, testing their restlessness: No one moved. "We must forge an independent Irish political party whose members are pledged to sit, act, and vote together. Handled properly, such a party could virtually stop Parliament from functioning. We will get reform."

There was silence in the room, then Michael Walsh spoke impatiently, "I don't care what you do in London, Dacre, the fact remains that the only thing the English understand is force. No fact has been more deeply stamped on the Irish than the realization that we can do nothing with an English government unless we frighten it."

"Precisely. What I am suggesting, Mr. Walsh, is that you move your field of operation from the hillside to Westminster." He looked around and suddenly his pleasant voice cut like edged glass. "Ireland possesses neither armies nor fleets. Having neither armies nor fleets you are bound to rely on constitutional and parliamentary methods. There is no hope for Ireland in violence."

"But is there hope for Ireland in Westminster? The answer to that, it seems to me, depends on what you mean by land reform, Duke." John Farrell, solid, stocky and, after Murdoch, the critical man whom Dacre had to convince, spoke for the first time. "Perhaps you will tell us your ideas on that subject, Your Grace."

"I should be happy to," Dacre said agreeably. "The immediate problem is to settle the rack rent problem and halt the evictions. Then we need to open up more

118

land and give the people a chance to acquire property that will belong to no one but themselves."

Christina was aware of the shock of surprise that ran around the room. They had not expected this.

"How?" It was Murdoch's voice, but he spoke for them all.

"The second problem is the easiest," Dacre spoke slowly. "There are nearly three million acres of bogland known to exist: I would like to see it reclaimed and made available for peasant purchase through government loans; I would like to see a drainage act for cultivated land; the major problem in this country is that there is not enough land for the population. Obviously, as a corollary to all this, we need to provide a way of making a living off the land. Irish manufacture needs to be stimulated. As to the rack rent problem, here we are treading on tender ground. Parliament is composed of landowners who will hardly be amenable to laws which cut away their own privileges. But when landowners abuse their responsibilities to the degree that has happened in Ireland, then, clearly, action must be taken. I would propose a land court system which would be empowered to fix a fair rent; that rent, so fixed, would then stand for fifteen years."

Dacre looked at the five men who had gathered to pass judgment on him. "Well, gentlemen," he said quietly, his strong, slender hands lying interlaced and still on the table, "do you approve?"

In the brief silence that followed, Christina fought and conquered an impulse to add her voice to her husband's. But this was Dacre's program and they had to accept him on his own credibility if he were to lead at all.

Murdoch's intense blue eyes looked at the faces of his colleagues, then he spoke. "What do you want us to do?" he said simply.

Dacre's still hands moved slightly, the only sign he

119

gave of the tension he had been under. For the first time since they had begun, he turned to his wife and a smile fleetingly appeared in his eyes. "Christina?"

She leaned forward, effortlessly capturing their attention. "Once we get Catholic Emancipation, we will need candidates to contest every seat in Ireland as it becomes available. And, what is more to the point, we need to get those candidates elected. The forty-shilling freeholder has the vote here in Ireland. That means that anyone who owns a few sticks of furniture can vote; in this, at least, we have more freedom than the English."

"I do not think so, Christina," said Murdoch soberly. "You know as well as I that the landlords own the peasant's vote. If they defy their landlords, they stand the risk of eviction. And eviction in this country is as good as a sentence of death."

"That is how things stand now, Murdoch," Christina said. "We must change them." She continued with cold clarity, "We need to organize, to make Catholic Emancipation a symbol linked to land reform. Once the Bill is passed, we will be able to organize in the open. On the local level, use the priests." She paused, and looked slowly around the table. "Charles is asking that we do nothing less than organize a Catholic political nation. I think we can."

"We can damn well try," said John Farrell. And there was a murmur of agreement among the others.

Dacre looked at the faces of the five men in front of him. They were of different shapes and different ages, but they all had a look he recognized. It was the same look he had seen often on Christina's face: the look of someone who knew what had to be done and would count no cost to achieve it. The look of someone whose heart and mind were at one with each other. It was not a look he had seen often in government circles.

"Why are you doing this, Duke? For Christina?" It was Sean Molloy, asking the same question Murdoch had voiced at Strands. There was a brief, nerve-rending silence as Dacre's cool green eyes rested on Molloy's face. Then, apparently, he decided to answer. His voice was quite impersonal as he said, "Partly, of course. But ultimately, you know, it is in England's interest to have this Union work. A contented and prosperous Ireland will be of far greater benefit to us than an Ireland in constant turmoil and unrest. If we don't begin to heal the breach now between Protestant and Catholic, our failure will come back to haunt us I am doing it out of simple self-interest, gentlemen"

Murdoch's blue eyes, alarmingly, blazed into laughter. "It is an irresistible thought: an English Protestant aristocrat with a peasant Catholic nation behind him."

Dacre suddenly smiled and for the first time they felt the effect of the apparently effortless charm he could exert at will. "Irresistible, Mr. Lynch. I hope it is."

The meeting broke up shortly after that, with Christina and Dacre returning to Mallon House. She was understandably pleased by the outcome of their morning in Wicklow. Only one discordant note had been struck: Dacre's last speech to Sean Molloy. After mulling it over all afternoon, she broached the subject to Dacre as they were dressing for dinner. He had come in to see if she was ready, and she dismissed her maid and turned to look at him. He was dressed in a black coat that fitted his broad shoulders as if it had been molded on him; his shirt was an immaculate white.

He came forward and, taking the diamond pendant from her hands, clasped it around her throat. "There. Now, what do you want to say to me, Christina?"

Her hands briefly touched the pendant lying on her breast. "What you said to Sean this morning, Charles, did you mean it?"

121

"Which of my many statements are you referring to?"

"When you told him that it was in England's interest to make the Union work." There was a faint line between her level brows. "You really mean that, don't you, Charles?"

"I do. It is the basis of all my actions toward Ireland." He put his hand under her chin and tipped her face up to look at him. "Why should that trouble you, little eagle?"

"Because I feel as though I'm lying to you," she said frankly. "No one in that room today thinks the Union will work. And I feel like a cheat pretending to you that it will."

He took his hand from under her chin and stepped back, continuing to regard her gravely. "Why won't it work, Christina? It has worked with the Scots and the Welsh."

"They are Protestants." She rose and went to the window, where she stood for a minute looking out on Dublin. "It took my father a long time to come to this point, Charles. And I too have reached the same conclusion. In the political division of Europe which followed the Reformation, England and Ireland were left on opposing sides. That is an historical fact, and nothing can change it. We can never be one nation. The only question remaining is, will our separation come about as the result of peaceful evolution, which is the path you are setting us on, or will it come as the result of violence."

He spoke quietly. "Why are you telling me this?"

"Because I cannot accept your help under false pretenses. We need you. The meeting this morning only made clear to the others what I have known all along. But if we succeed, if *you* succeed, I do not think the resolution will be what you hope. After land reform

122

there will be a push for an Irish Parliament where Catholics can sit, and then for independence."

"Perhaps you are right, Christina. You know your countrymen as I do not. But the course we are presently headed on with Ireland is disastrous. Ahead lies only violence, hatred, and, if the potato crop ever fails, starvation. An independent Ireland with cultural and economic ties to England would be better than that."

Her smile was radiant. "Murdoch was right, Charles. You are a statesman."

Dacre smiled ruefully. "Ireland has been the downfall of better men than I. Let us just hope all goes according to plan."

Chapter Twelve

But purer than a tall candle before the Holy
   Rood
Is Cathleen, the daughter of Houlihan.
                    —William Butler Yeats

London was usually quiet in November, but the war
was going badly and Pitt convened Parliament early,
bringing back to town the governing elite of the country. Lady Camden gave a ball to open this "unofficial"
season, and it was at this gathering of the English
ruling class that Christina made her debut into society.
   Camden House was glittering with light as the Dacre carriage pulled up to the door. At the top of a
sweeping curve of staircase stood the Countess of
Camden, glittering with diamonds, receiving her
guests. The major-domo's voice seemed unduly loud
to Christina, as he announced the stream of visitors:
Lord and Lady Rinsdale...The Right Honorable Mr.

Elton... and then it was their turn: "His Grace the Duke of Dacre and Her Grace the Duchess." Christina smiled and turned, with Dacre's hand comforting and steady under her arm, and entered the ballroom.

The first person to see them enter was Lady Maria Rochdale, who had seen Dacre's bright head before he was announced. Her small, slender body was stiff as she watched the door, anxious to see the woman whom Dacre had made his wife.

Inevitably, her mind went back to their last meeting. She had been angry and deeply hurt by the brief note he had sent, announcing his marriage. But he had promised to call on her, and Maria, who had had great hopes of being the next Duchess herself, resolved at least to maintain her present position in his life.

Until, that is, she saw him.

It was a warm July afternoon when her butler announced him. She had felt her heart begin to hammer, but she schooled her face to stillness and gave permission for the Duke to be brought to her. Her first thought as she saw him in the doorway was: He has changed. He seemed brighter, fined down, stripped of his boredom and his laziness. His presence had always been commanding, but he had never looked like this. She grasped the back of a chair.

"You are looking well, Maria," he said gravely. And when she did not answer, "Shall I go away?"

She drew herself to her small height and spoke with dignity, "Of course you must stay, Charles, and have some refreshment." As he moved toward her over the thick rug, she rang a bell. "What will you have?"

"A glass of sherry, thank you."

"Sherry for His Grace and tea for me," she told the silent-footed servant. As the door closed behind the footman, she turned to Dacre. "Do sit down, Charles.

125

You must be uncomfortably warm after your long drive. You came from London, I collect?"

He came across the room toward her. "Yes, I came from London." She gestured him to a sofa and seated herself, determined not to be the one to open the topic that was on both their minds. He looked faintly amused. "You are as well bred as you are beautiful, Maria."

At that her blue eyes flashed, and her resolve broke. "Thank you, Charles. But for all that you have married someone else."

Suddenly, he was deadly sober. "That, Maria, is why I came to see you today." His tone sent a warning through her system, but she chose to ignore it.

"Lord Ardsley said you saved the government from possible civil war by halting Lady Christina," she said breathlessly. "It was a noble act, Charles. Everyone says so."

Under his thick gold lashes, she saw the sudden glint in his green eyes. She had made him angry and her hands clasped together nervously. The door opened and into the suddenly quiet room came a servant with a tray of refreshments. By the time wine and tea had been poured, the sudden tenseness her last words had produced had gone.

When they were alone again, Dacre put his glass on the delicate table next to the sofa and spoke steadily. "Maria, between us there has always been affection, I believe, as well as a good deal of kindness." He spoke carefully, his deep voice sounding a tocsin to her hopes. "It would be easier, perhaps, to leave my marriage in the terms of Lord Ardsley: an act of political expediency, nothing more."

"But it is something more, is it not?"

"Yes," he said gently.

"And you have come to tell me that what was between us is over."

"Yes," he had said again.

So now Lady Maria Rochdale looked with mixed feelings toward the doorway where Dacre's wife would appear.

When the Duke and Duchess of Dacre were announced, Lady Maria's were not the only eyes to swing curiously to the doorway. As always, Dacre's bright head, towering over the rest of the company, commanded instant attention. He looked both powerful and elegant in his perfectly cut black coat and immaculate knee breeches. But it was Christina who drew the eyes of the glittering assembly.

She wore an Empire sheath gown of pure white, its edges trimmed in an intricate design of gold. The long fall of sheer material from its high waist emphasized her tall slenderness and the low-cut bodice revealed a neck whose delicate loveliness was circled by a breathtaking diamond necklace. Diamonds also hung from her ears and flashed like stars in her high-piled silver hair. With Dacre's arm under hers, she advanced further into the room and the light from the great chandelier caught and illuminated her face.

There was a sharp intake of breath and a murmured expletive behind Lady Maria. She turned and found herself looking at Lord Henry Chatsworth. His dark, aquiline face held an expression it was not difficult for Maria to identify; his brown eyes looked dazed. "She is like a goddess," he said to Maria's raised eyebrows, and moved, as though drawn by a magnet, toward the crowd surrounding the Duke and Duchess.

Later in the evening Lady Maria saw him dancing with Christina, the same expression still on his face.

Lord Henry was the heir to a famous title and a considerable fortune. He was twenty-four years of age and held the parliamentary seat for his family borough; when his father died he would move to the House of

Lords. But government was not Lord Henry's keenest interest. He was a sportsman, a Corinthian, and to be admitted into the circle of his friendship was the dearest hope of all the aspiring young bluebloods in town. His most intimate friends were three of the richest, most well-connected young men in England: Mr. Henry Grant, Sir Henry Aldwyck, and Lord George Carlton. They were known as the Four Horsemen and all were prime catches in London's highly competitive marriage market.

Christina danced with them all.

She danced with the Earl of Camden, the Duke of Devonshire, Lord Francis Tregare, the Earl of Ardsley, and countless others whom she had difficulty remembering.

Dacre was pleased. He did his own share of dancing and spent some time in private conversations which he hoped would prove fruitful. Halfway through the evening he was standing in front of one of the ballroom's long windows watching Christina dance with Lord Henry, his eyes faintly amused, when he was joined by Mr. George Mowbray.

"Hallo, Charles. I arrived late—too late to catch your entrance." His blue eyes followed Christina's dancing figure, then returned to his friend. "I believe you once told me that all I needed to understand your marriage was to see your wife. You were right."

Dacre smiled. "Would you like to meet her?"

"It would give me great pleasure," Mowbray answered soberly, and followed Dacre across the polished boards of the dance floor.

Christina was equally pleased to meet Mr. Mowbray. Dacre had spoken of him as a friend and that appeared to be a title he bestowed on very few. He invited her to dance, but she preferred to sit and talk. It was a welcome respite in an otherwise peripatetic

128

evening. She liked him and invited him to tea. He accepted with alacrity.

Going home in the carriage that morning, Christina flexed her sore feet and yawned hugely. "And I used to think the English were soft," she said wonderingly. "Do they do that often?"

"Several times a week, at least," he answered.

"What!"

"And when there isn't a ball, there's a political reception."

She stared at him owlishly, then resolutely closed her eyes. "Perhaps I won't be invited," she muttered.

His deep voice was warm with amusement. "Oh, you'll be invited," he said. "Little eagle, you are a success."

Chapter Thirteen

> ... though now it seems
> As if some marvelous empty sea-shell flung
> Out of the obscure dark of the rich streams
> And not a fountain, were the symbols which
> Shadows the inherited glory of the rich
> —William Butler Yeats

Dacre's words were all too true, as Christina soon discovered. Her day usually began at ten with a gallop in the Park and ended at a ball at three in the morning.

"Unless they are dying, no one ever stays home," she complained to Dacre. "I am beginning to feel nostalgic about the easy days of campaigning in Kerry."

He merely smiled. "You are campaigning now. You may not be talking about the Emancipation Bill, but you will be swaying votes none the less."

"I know," she said tartly. "They're all like your Aunt Augusta—astonished that I speak real English."

"That's not fair, Christina. I thought you liked quite a few people."

"I do. I like George Mowbray, and the Harrys...." The Harrys were what Christina called the Four Horsemen.

"Speaking of the Harrys," Dacre interrupted, "have they actually moved in yet, or are they technically still visiting?"

Christina knew perfectly well what he meant, but she gave him her sweetest, most mystified smile. "They're just nice boys, Charles. They remind me a bit of Liam Emmet." They were eating dinner before leaving for a reception, and she looked very beautiful in a dress of pale green silk.

Dacre shook his head. "I suppose you know that they have taken to wearing a piece of green ribbon in the buttonholes of their coats?"

Her mouth deepened at the corners. "I know."

"You are a femme fatale, love. Just be careful not to start any fires you don't want to quench."

Christina put down her fork and stared at him in astonishment. "I? A femme fatale? I am nothing of the sort, Charles."

"The ones who don't realize it are the worst kind," he said enigmatically. Then, as she continued to stare at him, "Eat your dinner, Christina. We'll be late for Lady Ashton's reception."

If Christina was busy, so was Dacre. When they were not visiting, they were entertaining: to Dacre House came men of riches, rank, broad acres, ancient lineage, and political influence. As she watched Dacre in this company, Christina began to fully realize the power and the respect he commanded. In the small, elite society of landowners and rulers that comprised the British Parliament, Dacre was clearly a commanding figure. These weeks in London showed her another side of Dacre's complex character: That under his cool, controlled exterior there boiled deep passions she already knew, but the cold-blooded thoroughness and steely will that he exhibited in the forging of a majority vote for Emancipation was something she had not quite been prepared for. And she found it difficult to reconcile the articulate, dangerous politician, whose words, according to Lord Hampton, had the same effect on his opponents as a bullet on a bubble, with the engaging companion whose effortless charm was no small asset in determining his influence.

There was one other thing Christina noticed about Dacre during the weeks before the first Parliament of the United Kingdoms of Great Britain and Ireland met: He was enjoying himself.

"I suppose I am," he admitted to her one evening as they were dressing to go out to another reception. "It must be the influence of you and your Irish friends, but I find it is satisfying to work unconditionally for something one believes in. It makes for a nice change."

"From what I can see," she said lightly, "the English believe in one thing only: the pursuit of their own pleasure. All else is secondary."

He frowned. "Surely not, Christina. There are many serious and brilliant men in England. Do not rate us so lightly."

"That may be so, Charles, but they are not serious or brilliant enough to see the unspeakable disaster their rule has brought upon the people of Ireland. Or, for that matter," and she put down again the cloak she had just taken up, "to see the squalid throng of destitute outcasts that people their own capital. Some of the sights I have seen in London are easily equal to the worst Ireland has to offer."

There was a minute's silence, then Dacre picked up Christina's cloak and put it around her shoulders.

132

"As always, little eagle, you are right," he said evenly. "Shall we go?"

Dacre was thinking of this conversation a few nights later when he was sitting over port with Father John Connolly, the priest who had married them. Christina had invited Father Connolly to dinner one night and Dacre, much to his own surprise, had found he liked the slender, scholarly priest very much. They had met several times after that, as Christina usually drove out to Kensington on Sundays to attend mass, and Dacre had gone once or twice and stayed to talk to Father Connolly.

On this particular evening they were alone at Dacre House, Christina having gone to a Ball under George Mowbray's escort. "Don't worry, Charles," Mowbray had assured him, "I will take care to protect Her Grace from the clutches of the Four Horsemen."

Dacre had merely smiled. "I am, of course, pleased that she is so popular, but it can become—ah—a little wearing."

He was remembering the picture Christina had made as she went out the door on Mowbray's arm, her high-piled hair silver in the moonlight, and remembering also her opinion of the people she was going to socialize with, as he sat across the fireplace from John Connolly in the library of Dacre House. They had been looking at some of Dacre's first editions, but now he closed the book he was holding and, his face wiped clean of all expression, addressed the priest.

"How do you like living in England, Father? Do you miss Ireland at all?"

"Sometimes," the priest answered slowly. "But my order has sent me here and, really, it has been no hardship. I like the English."

There was a barely perceptible flicker on Dacre's

133

face. "I had hoped Christina would feel that way, too. After all, now that we are one nation——"

He stopped as the priest's head snapped up. His thin face was intense as he stared across at the firelit figure of Dacre. "You misunderstand me, Your Grace," he said deliberately. "I said I liked your people, and so I do, but I shall never think of an Englishman as my countryman. I should as soon think of applying that term to a German." His words hung in the air and he saw the face across from him harden and change.

"Nevertheless," said Dacre grimly, "it is the Union of our two countries that offers Ireland her best hopes for improving the living conditions of her people."

"Christina has confided in me a little," Father Connolly said, "enough for me to understand that you are going to try to win land reform legislation from the new Parliament." He hesitated, then said carefully, "I do not want to discourage you, Your Grace, but I wonder if you realize what the repercussions of any movement toward land reform will be in Ireland."

"I think I have a very good idea, Father."

"I hope so. There is no such thing as genuine loyalty to England in Ireland, Your Grace. There is a separation of the Irish people into two hostile camps: one Protestant, the other Catholic. The Catholics, who have historically been robbed and oppressed by the English, have naturally no feelings of good will toward your country. That might change if they are given genuine concessions by the British Parliament. But the Protestants...." Father Connolly trailed off and looked skeptically at Dacre.

A log cracked and flared in the fire, casting a momentary glow over the Duke's still face. "The Protestants, Father Connolly, govern Ireland as a bureaucracy drawing authority from the King of England." The Duke's voice was deep and uninflected as he went on, his eyes on the priest's face. "They cannot cast him off without casting off their own ascendancy, which is why they have remained loyal for so long. But let the English government make a step toward redressing the grievances of the Catholic majority, and the Protestant garrison will revolt."

The priest's eyes were thoughtful. "You *do* know what you're dealing with."

"I think so. And the only way the English government is going to redress those Catholic grievances is if the alternative to Protestant threats is a breakdown in the very process of government."

"I see. It seems that at this point in time, our circumstances place a premium on political ability. If you will lead us, then perhaps there is hope in this Union. But, Your Grace, it will take many years for the scars to heal. Lady Christina is managing very well, I think. Don't expect too much of her. She needs more time."

Lines of fatigue softened the hardness of Dacre's arrogant mouth. "I know," he said. "I know."

They went to Dacre's Sussex estate for Christmas. The house, built by Dacre's father, was a jewel of eighteenth-century architecture, with an Adam staircase and columns, and miles of perfectly landscaped park. For three weeks Dacre relaxed, giving rein to the country-gentleman part of his character, exercising his horses and his dogs, caring for his estates and the people who lived on them, administering justice from the local bench.

Christina, too, enjoyed the quieter days and nights, the deeper intimacy that the country afforded them. It was with something like regret that she accompanied Dacre back to London for the opening of Parliament.

On January 28, Dacre attended a levee at St. James's Palace. He returned home at six o'clock and went directly to Christina's sitting room. She looked up from her book and cried out when she saw his face "It is all over," he said. "The King swears he will never consent to Catholic Emancipation."

Chapter Fourteen

Now days are dragon-ridden, the nightmare
Rides upon sleep....

—William Butler Yeats

Christina was sitting at her desk, writing to Murdoch Lynch. The beautiful lines of her mouth were as grim as they could ever be, her hand remained steady only with great effort. "Charles says Lord Loughborough is the villain," she wrote steadily. "Evidently he told the King that there was a movement for Catholic Emancipation being organized. Charles always distrusted Loughborough—there is something about him which even treachery cannot trust, he once told me. But Loughborough is, after all, the Lord Chancellor. They could hardly keep it from him. And he went straight to George, telling him with the deepest solicitude that such a bill would be against the King's coronation oath.

"Charles was at St. James's Palace on the 28th. The King was talking to Henry Dundas when he caught sight of Lord Castlereagh. 'What is it that this young lord has brought over which they are going to throw at my head?' he shouted. 'The most jacobinical thing I ever heard of! I shall reckon any man my personal enemy who proposes any such measure.' Charles said he was furious, his face all red, with the veins standing out.

"Pitt was not at the levee, and he and Charles consulted all night. The next day Charles went to see the King. George is adamant. He told Charles his coronation oath bound him to maintain the supremacy of the Church of England, and that those who held employments in the State must be members of it. Charles pushed him a bit, and he ended up shouting that he would rather give up his throne and beg his bread from door to door throughout Europe than consent to Catholic Emancipation.

"I rather like the idea of George as a beggar, but I'm afraid we can't count on it. Murdoch, I don't know what we are going to do. Charles relied on Pitt's being able to persuade the King. He always has in the past. Charles is meeting with Pitt right now...."

She heard voices downstairs, and put down her pen. In a few moments the door of her sitting room opened and Dacre himself came in. From polished head to shining boots, his grooming was faultless; but the green eyes were heavy and weariness sounded in the clipped notes of his voice. "We're finished, Christina," he said. "Pitt is resigning the Prime Ministership in protest."

The bone structure of her face looked suddenly more prominent under the clear young skin. Her eyes, North Atlantic gray, never left his face. She spoke through stiff, white lips. "Who is to be the next Prime Minister?"

There was a charged silence as he looked at her, sitting so straight-backed and still on her fragile chair. Dawning anger chased away the fatigue in his eyes. "Addington. Cornwallis, Castlereagh, and I resigned also. Did you really think I would take it?"

At the tone of his voice she cried out in protest. "No, Charles! I'm just so confused and upset, I don't know what to think."

His face had a sallow bleakness that frightened her. "I'll tell you what to think," he said. "The fight for Catholic Emancipation is over. Pitt has gone as far as he will for it. With the European situation being what it is, he will not take any extreme measures. And it will take very extreme measures indeed to compel the King to agree to Emancipation." He looked at her stricken face and his green eyes were lightless. When he spoke his voice was inflexible. "I will write to Murdoch Lynch, Christina. I want you to stay out of this."

The weeks that followed seemed to Christina a miasma of uncertainty and despair. Dacre was winding up affairs at the House and she scarcely saw him. For the first time since their marriage he had begun to use his own bedroom. He didn't want to disturb her, he said, when he came home late. But usually Christina was awake, lying with open eyes as she saw the light flare under the connecting door between their rooms. He never opened it. When they met occasionally at meals he was unfailingly polite, aloof, and unreachable.

The angles and hollows of Christina's face became more prominent as the weeks went by. She had canceled all their social engagements and saw very few people. Occasionally she let one of the Harrys coax her into taking a drive around the park and she went several afternoons to Kensington to see Father Connolly.

139

"Charles has become a stranger, Father," she said on her second visit. "I can't reach him. He absolutely refuses to discuss anything to do with Ireland with me." Her head was high as she looked at the sympathetic face of the priest. "I don't know what to do," she said hardly. "Do you have any suggestions?"

"Give him time, my child," Father Connolly said gently. "With one blow the King put an end to months of effort." The priest stirred his tea, then said slowly, "You and I, Christina, are used to failure. Being Irish, we were bred on it. We can't expect the Duke to be quite as resilient as we."

"Perhaps not," she agreed. "But I think only part of Charles's problems arise from his disappointment over the King's action. He is not the sort of man to let himself be thrown by one setback. If one door closed in his face, it would only spur him on to force open another one."

"That is probably true." Father Connolly put his cup down on the small table that separated him from Christina and regarded her gravely. "What is the Duke's problem, Christina?"

"There is only one door left, Father, and Charles does not want to force it," she said grimly.

In the room's sudden silence, she could hear the sounds of children playing in the yard next door. Finally the priest spoke. "The King, you mean?"

"Yes. Before we left Ireland in October, Michael Walsh said to Charles that we never have been able to do anything with an English government unless we frightened it. But we hoped, then, that we would at least be able to get Emancipation. The real fight would begin after that crucial point, when we would be able to send a Catholic Party to Parliament. But we will have to fight first for Emancipation, it seems."

"Which means open defiance of the King."

"Yes. In arms, perhaps."

His narrow face looked suddenly weary. "I can't blame the Duke, Christina. Ireland isn't his country."

Christina looked like a figure carved from porcelain as she sat in the shabby old wing chair in front of the fireplace. "I know," she said. "But it is mine."

Christina was thinking of Father Connolly's words as she dressed for dinner. As she allowed the maid to twist her shining hair into an elegant chignon and fasten a rope of pearls around her neck, the inner sensation she had of being torn in two actually caused the room to swim before her for a moment.

"Are you all right, Your Grace?" she heard her dresser asking anxiously.

"Yes, perfectly, thank you," she answered, getting herself under control with some difficulty.

"Perhaps you ought to lie down," the woman suggested.

"No," Christina said sharply. Dacre was to be home for dinner this evening, the first time in over a week. She wanted to talk with him. This was not the first momentary faintness she had experienced lately, and she thought she knew the reason for it. "I shall be fine," she said to her maid. The woman nodded understandingly.

Dacre was urbane and charming as their meal progressed. His good manners and easy chatter were as effective a barrier between them as a wall; Christina felt like throwing a crystal glass at his aloof, arrogant face. When he broached the subject of the Duchess of Devonshire's ball, which he wanted them to attend, Christina felt as if she had had enough.

"I would rather not, Charles," she said quietly. The footmen were dexterously removing the plates from the second course and Christina had eaten very little. She seldom felt hungry lately.

"Nonsense," he said coolly. "It will do you good to

get out. Brooding at home is no solution." He looked at her plate. "All this hanging about the house is making you lose your appetite. You need a little gaiety."

"I need," she said slowly and deliberately, "a husband who will stop sulking long enough to speak to me intelligently about the future of my country."

There was an inimical silence, then Dacre rose to his feet. "We have spoken about that, Christina, and the subject is closed. I shall expect to escort you to the Devonshire's Saturday evening." Then, as so often, lately, he was gone.

Christina was left sitting at the table, straight-backed and still, with only her stormy eyes an indication of the anguish and fury bottled up within her.

She went to the Devonshire Ball. It was her first social appearance since the defeat of the Emancipation Bill, and there were many eyes straining to catch sight of her face to see if it betrayed any emotion. They were all disappointed: It did not. But concern over a grave political problem, pain over her estrangement from Dacre, and guilt over a pregnancy she was not sure she wanted, had taken their toll. Christina was a tightly-wound spring about to shoot off at any minute. Her head hurt with the tension of it.

Lord Henry Chatsworth and his friends moved in to take care of her as soon as Dacre disappeared, which he did almost immediately. But Christina could not surmount the painful tension within. The inevitable explosion came about halfway through the evening.

The catalyst was Sir Francis Meldrun, a harmless old man who had always admired Christina. He came over to her just before supper was served and the orchestra was silent. He was more than a little deaf, and to Christina's sensitive nerves it seemed as though he were shouting at her. "My dear Duchess," he cried

142

genially, "what a pleasure to see you. Your absence in the last few weeks left quite a gap in our circle."

Christina looked from his smiling, well-bred, well-fed face to the glittering crowd assembled in the Duchess of Devonshire's ballroom, and she felt something give way within her. "It is very kind of you to say so, Sir Francis," she said with bell-like clarity, "considering that I am a Catholic."

"My dear Duchess," the old man shouted, distress in his face, "such a thing to say. As if that mattered."

"But it does matter, Sir Francis," she said evenly. "Injustice always matters, at least it does to the victim."

Sir Francis looked around wildly, clearly anxious for rescue from what was becoming an extremely difficult conversation. "Injustice," he boomed, "nonsense. We are all your friends here."

"Indeed," she responded coldly and her eyes swept around the suddenly silent room. "But your nation is not a friend of my nation."

"I believe, Your Grace," it was the elegant tones of Mr. Locke, undersecretary for Ireland, "that our nations have united into one kingdom; they are not separate entities any longer. And there are many benefits due to Ireland from this Union, I might add."

"Your Union, Mr. Locke, is nothing more than a brutal annexation unless you afford to the Irish the basic rights you yourselves enjoy under your famous English constitution." She raised her chin and stared at the richly-dressed aristocrats who surrounded her. Her words were bitter and serious: "Ireland is a Catholic country. If you wish to make a union with her you must admit Catholics into the process of government. Until you do that, you will be nothing but an alien and hostile garrison to whom we will never be reconciled. You can jail us, you can starve us, you can kill us, but you will never appease us." Across the room her eyes met her husband's. "Give us our rights," she said, her eyes still on his. "Make this Union a reality, not an empty shadow. For if you don't, rest assured that some-day we will throw you out of Ireland forever."

She dominated the room, the slender girl in her pale blue ball gown. The elegant and charming Duchess of Dacre had disappeared. Before them, with her un-tamed eyes and proud face, stood Christina Mac-Carthy. Instinctively, they stood back as she walked to the doorway. For Christina, the months of discipline and careful courtesy were over.

In the stunned silence that followed Christina's exit, Lord Henry Chatsworth turned to Dacre, who was standing beside him. He looked, Lord Henry thought, like a man who had been struck between the eyes. But the sound of Christina's exit had almost died away, and still Dacre did not move. His brilliant dark eyes flashing, Lord Henry turned from the Duke and stalked out in Christina's wake. He was followed faith-fully by his three friends.

By the time Christina got home with her escort, reaction was setting in. Lord Henry was very conscious of the shadows of fatigue under her winter-gray eyes, and did not insist on staying. It hurt him to leave her, unprotected against Dacre's anger, but he realized grimly that he had no choice. He knew too that under the fragile flesh and bone of Christina there lay a steely toughness probably greater than his own. He only said, "May I wait on you tomorrow?"

Christina smiled at him gratefully. "Yes, thank you, Harry." Her smile moved to include the three other young men standing at the foot of the stairs. "Thank you all. You are friends indeed."

She entered the house slowly and explained to a surprised butler than she had felt ill and Lord Henry had brought her home early. She let her maid undress her and put her to bed. But the hours ticked away and she did not sleep, lying still with her eyes fixed on the door which led to Dacre's bedroom.

Light was beginning to touch the sky when she heard his step outside her door. Her nerves felt bruised from the long wait and it was with difficulty that she kept silent as he threw open her bedroom door. He stayed still for a moment in the doorway, his eyes on the bed.

"Come in, Charles," she said quietly. "What took you so long?"

He closed the door and went to put a log on the fire. It flared up, brightening the whole room, and she was able to see him clearly. His green eyes were brilliant in a too-composed face, and for the first time Christina felt fear touch her. "Where were you?" she said breathlessly.

He ignored her question and crossed the polished floor toward her, his too-deliberate walk answering for him. He had been drinking. Her own eyes were dark in her pale, thin-boned face as she watched him come. "I meant what I said tonight," she told him.

"Indeed," he said pleasantly, his tone grating on her nerves. "And was it necessary to throw your defiance at the whole of society?"

"I think so," she said hardily. 'Someone has to tell them the truth."

He sat down beside her on the bed, his eyes thoughtful. "You might have considered the position you were placing me in, I think. After all, you are my wife." He was so close to her, she could feel the heat from his skin. "Aren't you my wife, Christina?" he said softly.

"Yes," her voice was barely audible.

His hand touched the fine-drawn skin over her cheekbone, then slid into her loosened hair. "Good," he murmured deeply and bent to kiss her.

Christina fought to smother her response, but
145

knew, as he lifted his head to look at her, that she had failed. She looked down at his beautiful, long-fingered hand lying so caressingly on her breast, then at his long, arrogant mouth, taut now with a mixture of desire and temper. She had not expected to have to fight him on these grounds. "If you do this, Charles," she said through an aching throat, "you will destroy us."

His eyes, densely green, met hers and suddenly there was something dark and dangerous in the room. His nearness was a torment to her. "There is no prison in the world that is worse than love," she said bitterly.

He winced as if she had struck him, and drew his hand away. Slowly he stood up, the firelight catching and lighting his brows and disordered hair, the tips of his thick, open lashes, and the glinting green of his eyes. He took two steps back from the bed, then turned abruptly and left the room. Christina, appalled by what she had seen in his face, buried her own in the refuge of her pillow and wept.

Dacre's need was for refuge also, somewhere private and dark where he would be safe from everything, even his own thoughts. But there was no such place, and, as he drank a pot of hot coffee in the library and the cushion of alcohol wore off, his thoughts became more and more unpleasant. He changed his clothes to topboots and buckskin breeches and went to the stable. Hyde Park was deserted at this early hour, but his horse's galloping hooves could not outpace the pressures that were building in his mind. Finally, he took refuge in the one place where he knew he could be alone with his thoughts, one of the reading rooms at the British Museum.

He sat at the table where he had spent so many satisfying hours in the past, his eyes on a map open before him, his composed profile an effective mask for the bitterness of his reflections. Over and over again

Christina's words reverberated through his mind: "There is no prison in the world that is worse than love."

The icy rage which had possessed him since the King's announcement was broken and he reviewed, silently, his past behavior and his future options. He did not like what he saw. He had treated Christina unforgivably, and the damnable thing was he didn't know how to make it up to her. There was only one thing that might force the King into agreeing to Catholic Emancipation: the threat of civil war. He could not lend himself to that; not while there was still hope that some reforms would be carried forward by Parliament. But Christina would not be satisfied by a few token parliamentary reforms; nor would Murdoch Lynch.

He had tried to break her, to force her to acknowledge her dependence on him, out of fear of losing her. Dacre's eyes looked bruised with fatigue as he pushed his chair back and slowly rose to his feet. The decision was hers to make. He would have to face her. Moving slowly, as though very tired, he left the museum to make the short trip across London to Dacre House and his wife.

Lord Henry Chatsworth had come to pay his promised visit to Christina. She greeted him with eyes darkly sleepless, and gestured him to a seat beside her. "I must thank you again for your escort last night, Harry," she said. "I only hope you won't suffer for your gallantry. What I said won't be forgiven, I am afraid."

His dark eyes flashed magnificently. "You were splendid. It's about time someone faced up to the bloody arrogance of the English ruling classes." He looked at her closely. "What did Dacre have to say?"

She looked, if possible, even darker about the eyes. "He was angry, of course," she said in a low voice.

He reached out impulsively and grasped her wrist. "Tell me what I can do for you," he demanded. "Do you want me to go to Ireland and fight for you? I will."

She shook her head. "Oh Harry, I am sorry. This is a situation between Charles and me. No one else can help."

Then, because she was so beautiful and looked so fragile and he loved her so much, he reached for her blindly. "Christina!" he said, his voice almost a moan, and sought her mouth with hard, demanding lips.

She remained perfectly still; passive and unresponsive in his hold. Suddenly a voice came across the room, quiet and deadly. "Chatsworth. Let go of my wife." Lord Henry released Christina abruptly and they both turned involuntarily to where Dacre filled the doorway.

"May I ask what is going on here?" he said, his voice extremely precise. With hammering heart, Christina realized that he was in a towering rage. Unbidden there flashed into her mind the image of Dacre standing over the dead body of Thomas Dibden. Instinctively, she stepped between the two men. She tried to meet Dacre's eyes, but suddenly there was a thick mist before her, obscuring her vision. She blinked hard to clear it, but the mist thickened until it blocked out all sight and sound. Quietly, she slipped to the floor.

Dacre leaped forward and picked up his wife's limp form, bringing her to rest on the sofa. His face was almost as white as hers as he bent over her, his fingers on her wrist. "Send for the doctor, Chatsworth," he ordered the young man over his shoulder, and Lord Henry leaped to obey. By the time he returned to the room, Christina was beginning to stir. Dacre spoke to her in a voice that Lord Henry had never heard from him before, and Christina murmured something in reply The Duke gathered his wife in his arms and lifted her gently. She let her head rest gratefully on his broad shoulder; her long lashes lay still on her cheek. Dacre spared a glance for Lord Henry. "Wait here for me," he said, and carried Christina from the room.

He returned in about ten minutes. "She seems to be all right," he told Lord Henry. "She is conscious. Her maid is with her. The doctor should be here momentarily."

"Thank God," Lord Henry said fervently.

"Yes." Dacre looked at the young, handsome face regarding him with a mixture of apology and defiance. Christina's faint had effectively dissipated Dacre's anger and he was able now to assess the situation as it really was. Astonishingly, he said to Lord Henry, "I am sorry."

Lord Henry found that something was interfering with his breathing. "I would do anything in the world for her," he managed to say.

"I know," Dacre said wearily. "So would I. Almost."

"It's you she loves." Raw pain sounded in the young man's voice. "She is worth anything, Dacre. Surely you know that."

The Duke's face looked haggard with suppressed emotion. "We're beginning to sound like a scene out of a bloody French tragedy, Chatsworth," he said brutally. "You'd better go before I challenge you to a duel or something equally futile." There was no amusement in Dacre's bleak look and Lord Henry took his leave in some confusion about the Duke's meaning. It wasn't until after dinner that evening that he realized Dacre must have been referring to Corneille, whose plots all dealt with a hero and heroine torn between love and duty.

The doctor arrived and spent about fifteen minutes with Christina. Then he went to the library to speak

149

to the Duke. "Her Grace is doing very well, now," the doctor told Dacre as he advanced into the magnificent book-lined room. "But I won't answer for her health unless she gets more rest than she has been getting lately. In her condition, rest is of the utmost importance."

Dacre's face had radically altered at the doctor's words. "Her condition?" he said carefully.

The doctor looked at him sharply. "Her Grace came to me a month ago. She is expecting a child."

Dacre looked stunned. "I didn't know."

The doctor's searching blue eyes traveled across the Duke's face. "Perhaps she was waiting for the right moment to tell you," he said. "But, Your Grace, it is essential that the Duchess avoid the kind of stress and worry that has obviously been plaguing her. She is a healthy young woman. I expect no complications. But she must have rest!"

Dacre nodded his understanding and in a few moments the doctor was gone. The Duke was stunned indeed. But, along with the surprise and worry, was a fierce joy that caught him more off guard than anything. It was many minutes before he felt composed enough to go and see his wife.

She was lying, still and white, on the high bed with her eyes closed. He saw as he came closer that under the dark lashes were blue stains of utter weariness. Remorse struck him like a blow.

"Christina," he spoke low. "Why didn't you tell me?"

Her lashes fluttered and eyes of winter gray looked at him. He took her hand. Her eyes traveled from his face down to where his long, narrow fingers held her own capable hand. "This last month has not been an easy time for us," she answered.

He took a deep breath. "No, it has not, and I must bear the blame for it." He put her hand down gently upon the blanket and walked to the window. He stood for a moment looking out at the deepening dusk, then turned and spoke to her with difficulty. "Let us be honest with each other, Christina. There is only one thing that will force the King to change his mind about Emancipation."

"Violence," she said quietly.

"Yes, violence; armed rebellion; the threat of civil war." He met her eyes, his own heavy and bruised looking. "I do not think that things have come to the point where I can countenance that. This Union may still be made viable through parliamentary action."

"How?" Her voice was barely a thread.

"By abolishing the separate executive for Ireland for one thing. That would break the Protestant Ascendancy."

"Will Addington do it?"

"I don't know," he spoke slowly. "I will talk to him, and to Portland, the new Home Secretary. I must give them time to act." He came back to stand at the foot of her bed. "That won't satisfy Murdoch Lynch, I know. But it is the best I have to offer."

She lay back on her pillows, her pale hair tumbled loose about her shoulders. The open neck of her night gown showed the rapidly beating pulse in her throat. "If Murdoch succeeds in putting enough pressure on the government to force the King to change his mind, then would you lead an Irish Party in Parliament?"

"Yes," he said simply.

Her hand went to her throat in a helpless, blind motion. "And what of the present? What will you do now?"

He looked at his hands as they grasped the bedpost, and answered, "Retire to Strands, run my estates. Write." He raised his eyes and regarded her calmly. "Watch my child grow."

Sudden color flamed like flags in her cheeks. Her thinking gray eyes searched his face. "Could you do that, Charles? Retire from the world you have helped to run for so long?"

He stayed where he was at the foot of the bed, and when he answered his voice was even. Only his whitened knuckles on the bedpost gave away his tension. "Yes," he said. "If you were with me."

In the sudden silence a log crackled and fell on the fire. Christina's eyes were smoke under the straight line of her brows. "There is nowhere else for me to go," she answered.

It was said; the choice had been made. The price of their union was a career and a nation, and the cost to both had been dear. But as their lips and bodies met and clung, neither regretted what they had done.

Chapter Fifteen

O but we dreamed to mend
Whatever mischief seemed
To afflict mankind, but now
That winds of winter blow
Learn that we were crack-pated
when we dreamed.

—William Butler Yeats

Dacre went to Westminster the next day to see the
Prime Minister and the Home Secretary. The sight of
his familiar bright head in the Lobby caused a minor
sensation among the members, but Dacre appeared to
be unconscious of anything unusual. His face was unreadable, a mask with veiled green eyes and charming
smile. No one cared to ask him what all were anxious
to know: What was he going to do now?

Dacre's meeting with Addington and Portland was
a study in diplomacy. Neither minister trusted Dacre

and both feared him. But the Duke's voice was cordial as he opened the subject he had come to discuss. "I would like to share with you gentlemen a few thoughts on the subject of Ireland. The welfare of the Irish people is of deep concern to my wife, as you know." He looked at Portland, who had been present at the Devonshire Ball, and the older Duke cleared his throat.

"We quite understand, Dacre. Now that Ireland is joined to us in a United Kingdom the welfare of the Irish people must naturally be of concern to His Majesty's Government as well."

"That is what I think, Your Grace," Dacre responded. "I have given this matter a great deal of thought since my resignation over the Emancipation Bill. If we do not want continuous disturbance in Ireland, it is essential to show the majority Roman Catholic population that we are interested in promoting a real union of our two nations. This is what I had hoped Emancipation would do." He watched the two men closely as he continued evenly, "However, there is one other thing we can do: Abolish the Lord Lieutenancy."

Portland's small eyes opened wide and he stared at Dacre suspiciously. "Why should we do that, Your Grace?"

"Ireland ought not to have a separate executive. The Lord Lieutenancy is both the symbol and the means of a continuing Protestant Ascendancy. The union of the Parliaments has transferred the power of legislation from Dublin to Westminster; but in all other respects, power still rests with the same people as before. In every department of government, central and local, the Protestant landlords and their dependents remain in control."

"The Protestant landlords, Your Grace, are at least loyal to the crown. I cannot say as much for the Catholics." Addington leaned forward across the table toward Dacre. "If we take away the authority of Dublin

154

Castle, we will throw the Protestants into rebellion as well."

Dacre's smile held no amusement. "I am glad you made that point, Mr. Addington. The Protestants are loyal to England so long as it is to their benefit. The Protestant Ascendancy is nothing more than the exploitation of English rule in the interests of the property, power, and promotion of the Irish landowners as against the Irish peasants." His eyes, so strangely green, were perfectly bleak as he regarded the two men facing him. "I do not think that such exploitation is to the benefit of either the Irish people or His Majesty's Government. And I fear that, unless we redress this serious wrong, one day the Irish masses, in all their incredible poverty and distress, will revolt in earnest."

There was a brief silence, then Portland said, "We must thank you for sharing your thoughts with us, Your Grace. May we hope for your continued assistance and advice?"

Dacre rose to his intimidating height and the two ministers rose with him. "I am afraid, Duke, that I will not be in a position to offer my thoughts. My wife and I are returning to Strands where we plan to make a long stay."

Addington's relief permitted him to smile humorously. "You won't be going to Ireland, then, Duke?"

Dacre did not smile in return. "No," he said. "Not yet."

With great effort, Addington refrained from looking at Portland until Dacre had gone. Then he turned to his Home Minister and said with feeling, "Damme."

"Yes," said Portland grimly. "It was a threat, all right. The question is, how far does he mean it?"

Dacre was driving through St. James's when he saw George Mowbray. At Mowbray's signal, he pulled his horses over to the curb.

"Hallo, Charles. I just got back to town this morning. How's the Duchess?"

Dacre looked at his friend's worried face and motioned him to climb into the curricle. "I can see you've already heard about the Devonshire Ball, George. Don't worry, Christina is fine."

"It was the first thing I heard when I got to town," Mobray confided. "I don't know who are noisier, the Duchess's champions or her detractors."

"Have you run into Lord Henry Chatham?"

"At Tattersalls, this morning." He looked shrewdly at the Duke. "It must have been a damned unpleasant evening, Charles."

"It was my fault," Dacre said. "I provoked her into it, then stood by and let her walk out by herself."

"So I heard," Mowbray said gently.

Dacre sighed. "Not one of my better evenings, George. In fact, it hasn't been one of my better months. Christina got the brunt of it and, being Christina, she fought back."

Mowbray said mournfully, "I think people wait for me to go out of town before they do anything really interesting."

Dacre laughed, but dropped the topic of the Devonshire ball. "Speaking of going out of town, George, Christina and I are going home to Strands."

"A good idea," Mowbray said. "This thing will all blow over in a few weeks."

Dacre kept his eyes on the road ahead of him. "It really doesn't matter, George. We won't be coming back."

"What!" Mowbray jerked around to stare at Dacre's unyielding profile.

"I am retiring from public service, George. For good."

"I don't believe it."

"Nevertheless, it is true."

156

"Charles, think man. You've only had one setback. Are you going to throw away a brilliant career, a genuine chance to serve your country, because of one decision by the King?"

"I cannot serve the English Government, George, and remain married to Christina. I cannot ask her to aide and abet the advancement of a nation she regards as her enemy."

"But can you bury yourself, either? A landed gentleman of title and wealth, employing the passing days counting your sheep and mending fences for your tenants?"

"It won't be as bad as that, George."

"Perhaps not, but that is not the point." Mowbray was deeply agitated. "You are a leader, Charles. You have abilities that you haven't even tapped yet. To what do you owe your allegiance? What of your country?"

"And what of my wife? And my child?" Dacre looked at the startled expression on Mowbray's face and nodded. "Yes, my child. Do I not owe my family quiet mind and undivided loyalties as well?"

Mowbray was silent as Dacre drew up in front of his lodging. "I have thought about this long and hard, George. This is the only way."

Mowbray swung down to the curb in silence, a deeply perturbed expression on his face. "Don't take it so to heart, George," Dacre said kindly. "England can't afford me at the moment, anyway." With which cryptic words he drove away.

Before they left for Strands, Christina went to Kensington to see Father Connolly. He was hearing confessions and she waited for him in his small sitting room, the perfect stillness of her posture belying the tautness of her nerves. She rose when he came in and accepted his offer of tea, grateful for the delay. But finally the cups had been brought and the tea poured, and the priest's narrow, intelligent face was turned inquiringly toward her. She straightened her spine and began.

"Have you by any chance heard about the Devonshire ball, Father?"

"My housekeeper has a sister who works for the Duchess," he said gently.

Christina nodded. "Yes, well at least it broke the barrier between Charles and me. As we had agreed earlier, Charles feels that the only thing that will force the King to change his mind on Emancipation is the threat of civil war."

"And the Duke cannot, in all conscience, help to organize civil war in Ireland."

Christina looked him straight in the face and her cold, pure, young voice was remorseless. "I want you to write to Murdoch Lynch, Father. I want you to tell him how things stand with us. First, Charles cannot agree to join in any agitation to force the King to change his mind about Emancipation. He has made certain recommendations to the Cabinet and if those recommendations are met, he will feel satisfied that England is doing its best to fulfill the terms of the Union. Under these circumstances, Charles will retire from government for good. We will live at Strands and pursue our own lives, and we will hope to be allowed to do this by all our friends."

The priest looked at the flawless, lamp-lit face of the girl sitting opposite him. The clean, delicate bone structure, the clear young skin, the silver and rose coloring, all beautiful in themselves, were vessels only for the fierce, bright spirit of the character within. "I see," he said quietly. "And what if the government ignores the Duke's recommendations and continues on its present ill-advised course in Ireland?"

The corners of Christina's mouth deepened. "Tell

158

Murdoch," she said carefully, "that, under those circumstances, Charles has agreed to lead an Irish Party in Parliament. But we must first get Emancipation, or there will be no Irish Party."

"In other words, Christina," the priest's voice was uninflected, "Murdoch must mobilize the Irish masses in order to force the King's hand. And he must do this without you and without the Duke."

Christina's face was ice. "Yes."

"You have made your choice, I see, my child."

"Yes," Christina repeated, her voice definite, but this time the strain of the interview showed in the lines of her mouth.

"We will all respect it," he answered her. "I will write to Murdoch." He rose and went to stand beside her chair. He looked down into the grave, wide eyes of the last of Ireland's chiefs and said soberly, "Only good can come out of love, Christina. We must pray that God will show us the right path to take."

After she had left he sat down to write to Murdoch Lynch. And because he put very little faith in the foresight of the British government, the news he had to impart was cautiously optimistic.

Chapter Sixteen

Out of Ireland have we come
Great hatred, little room,
Maimed us at the start.
I carry from my mother's womb
A fanatic heart.

—William Butler Yeats

Murdoch Lynch sat in front of a peat fire in a cottage on the outskirts of Dublin waiting for his chosen leaders to arrive. Before him on the table were three letters. He planned to read them the one from Dacre, and the one from Father Connolly. He picked up once again the brief note from Christina. In her firm, precise writing he read for the twentieth time, "Dear Murdoch, I am sorry. As Liaden once said: *'Deilm ndega ro thethainn mo chridese; ro-fess nicon bia cena.'*" His blue eyes, so startling in his narrow, dark face, held an indefinable expression of pain. Suddenly, he crumpled

160

the letter and flung it into the fire. But the words of the great medieval love lament burned in his mind long after the flames had transformed the paper into ashes: "A blast of flame has pierced my heart. Most certainly, it will not endure without him," Christina had written. Murdoch shaded his eyes with his hand and continued to stare into the fire until he heard the voice of John Farrell at the door.

There were five men gathered in the cottage on that blustery March day. The same four whom Dacre had met and Father Cormac Burke, a priest from Galway who was active in local peasant associations. Murdoch's intense blue eyes looked at the sober faces of the men who were seated around him and he spoke deliberately. "We are gathered today to discuss the strategy necessary to force the King of England to accept Catholic Emancipation." Not one eye flickered and Murdoch picked up a paper that lay in front of him. "I wish first to read to you a communication I have had from the Duke of Dacre."

Murdoch opened the folded paper and read slowly, "My dear Lynch, I am afraid the King has put an end to all of our plans for placing an effective Irish Party in Parliament. Considering His Majesty's firm stand on the question of Catholic Emancipation, I feel my only option is to withdraw from the government and, indeed, from public life altogether. You have my good wishes for success in your future efforts for Ireland but, under the circumstances, I can hardly join with you. I shall, in future, be merely a private citizen, interested, but not involved, in affairs of state." Murdoch looked up from the writing to the faces watching him so intently. "It is signed Charles Standish, Duke of Dacre."

There was a passionate silence, then Liam Emmet

said furiously, "But what of Christina? Does she go along with this?"

Murdoch's smile was wintry. "I think I had better read you Father Connolly's letter next. He has several messages of interest." In a level, expressionless voice Murdoch proceded to read the priest's communication to the assembled company. There was absolute silence as he reached the concluding paragraph: "Either of two things might occur to bring the Duke back into our orbit. The first is, of course, your success in pressuring the King to accept an Emancipation Bill. Secondly, the chances of the Government's ignoring the Duke's sound advice are extremely high. Equally high is the chance of them doing something incredibly brutal and stupid that would provoke Dacre into taking action. I have had an opportunity to get to know him somewhat and he is a man with a highly developed sense of justice; I do not think we have lost him.

"My last advice is this: Leave Christina alone. This decision is tearing her apart. And she is expecting a child. Concentrate for the present on Ireland and leave things to work their way out here."

Murdoch looked up from the paper in his hands. "So it appears that we are on our own for the present, my friends. The question now is, what shall we do next?"

"Dacre, with his usual bloody insight, has told us what we have to do," said Michael Walsh bitterly. "'Civil war,' he said according to Father Connolly. And then he proceeded to take away the only trump card we have: Lady Christina. The people might rise to follow her. Without her, we haven't a chance."

The slow, deliberate voice of John Farrell interjected, "The Duke said something else in our meeting with him that sticks in my mind now: Ireland has neither armies nor fleets. Even if the people would rise for a rebellion, we all here must recognize the great responsibility of hurling our unarmed people on the points of British bayonets."

Liam's brown eyes were stormy. "Oh, Dacre was very persuasive. We all busily agreed with him, like a parcel of bishops before the Pope. But he was wrong. Thanks to him, Christina is lost to us——"

"Thanks to him, Christina is alive," Murdoch interrupted quietly. The older man's steady blue eyes met Liam's passionate dark ones and it was the younger man who dropped his gaze.

"All right, Murdoch," he said. "What do you suggest we do?"

Murdoch placed his hands on the table before him and regarded them intently. "One aspect of Dacre's plan that appealed to me when he broached it, and still does appeal to me, is the fact that it is legal. Acting in accord with the constitution means we do not have to worry about; one, informers, always a serious problem; and two, imprisonment, which in the past has so often deprived us of our most crucial leaders." He glanced around at their surroundings and then at the door, which was guarded by the cottage's owner, another veteran of '98. "We would no longer have to meet in secret," he said slowly.

"But Murdoch, the Duke's plan has failed," said Sean Molloy. "We all know its advantages; that is why we agreed to it in the first place. But it is no longer feasible."

Murdoch's eyes went back to his hands. "Part of it has failed," he said softly. "But not the basic idea. 'We are talking about a massive, constitutional movement,' Dacre said. Well, Ireland has constitutional rights the King cannot deny. What we need to do," said Murdoch with extreme precision, "is to organize a legal protest movement. We need to hold mass meetings of the people to talk about land reform and about Emancipation. We need to mobilize the political awareness of the people, and to do so in a way that cannot be dealt with as treason."

Farrell's heavy brows were drawn together. "Will the people respond to such a movement?"

"Land reform is the key. If we link land reform to the idea of Emancipation, I believe they will." He turned to Father Cormac Burke. "We will start with the county organizations, and I hope to rely upon the support of the clergy. The one thing London fears is an organized peasantry."

"There is serious unrest in the country at present," said Michael Walsh. "Agrarian violence is on the upswing once again. Are we to try to divert it to legal channels?"

Murdoch and John Farrell exchanged glances and it was Farrell who answered. "I think not. Large, organized mass meetings will be much more effective seen against the backdrop of peasant unrest and violence."

There was silence in the small room as the five men digested what had been said so far. Then, "How do we start?" said Liam Emmet.

Murdoch picked up a pen. "I'll tell you," he said, and proceeded to outline his plan in precise detail. There were very few questions and when the meeting broke up after two hours, each man knew clearly what he was expected to do.

"If only we had Lady Christina," said Michael Walsh as he prepared to leave. "Half of this work would be unnecessary, if she was joined with us."

Liam Emmet and Murdoch Lynch, who loved her, closed ranks against the man in the doorway. "Christina has already done more than her share," said Liam belligerently.

"Father Connolly is right," said Murdoch. "We must leave her alone. She deserves some peace."

"She won't have it, though," said Sean Molloy quietly, "until she comes home. And it is up to us to bring her. We must organize."

John Farrell rose and stumped to the door. "Aye, we must do our jobs, and trust to God for the rest."

Thus began one of the greatest constitutional movements in history. Under the aegis of a "Catholic Society," which ostensibly aimed to promote concord among all classes of Irishmen, a perfectly legal aim since it professed to be a social and not a political group, meetings were organized around the country. Attendance was small at first, but soon enthusiasm spread among the people, who felt for the first time that their leaders were talking about something that actually touched their lives. By the end of May the meetings were attracting hundreds of people, and by June thousands.

Even the members of the Central Committee of the Catholic Society were astonished by their success. "It's the issue, John," Murdoch told a bewildered John Farrell. "In ninety-eight we were talking about freedom, about a separate nation, political revolution. It meant nothing to the average peasant. But land reform, now that is something else."

By July the situation in Ireland had reached alarming proportions. The old specter of agrarian crime had reared its ugly head again and added to that was the legal agitation of the Catholic Society.

"The country is in a state of smothered war," wrote the Lord Lieutenant to the Duke of Portland. "We have no strength here but our army. Ireland, in a view to military operations, must be considered as an enemy's country."

On July 10 the Duke of Portland and the Prime Minister sat down to discuss the Irish situation.

"We must take some action, Mr. Prime Minister," said Portland. "The situation is serious."

"What does Lord Hardwicke say, Your Grace?"

"The Lord Lieutenant writes that within a few months every adult Catholic will be a member of this Society. There are seven million Catholics in Ireland, Addington! If they resort to arms, we will be helpless. We don't have the troops to spare to quell a rebellion of that size."

"Suppress the Society."

"How? It is a perfectly legal association."

Addington's lips compressed and he looked at Portland in frustration. "There must be something we can do! Has Hardwicke no suggestions?"

Portland's flat face was impassive. "According to Lord Hardwicke, the guiding spirit of this whole movement is a man called Murdoch Lynch. A man, I might add, that Cornwallis pardoned and released from jail only a year ago."

Addington's fist came down on the table. "Dammit man, then send him back to jail!"

"Under what charges, Mr. Addington?"

"Civil disorder. Habeas Corpus is suspended in Ireland under the terms of the Protection of Persons and Property Act. We can keep him in prison indefinitely. If he is indeed the force behind this new campaign, perhaps his removal will break it."

It was then that Portland broached the subject that was really troubling him. "What of Dacre, Mr. Addington? This Lynch was a follower of Niall MacCarthy. Will his arrest perhaps provoke Dacre into some kind of action?"

Addington pulled at his lip. "Damn the man. He hangs over us all like a bloody sword. He hasn't made any gestures toward Ireland, has he?"

"No, Mr. Prime Minister. He and the Duchess have been living quietly at Strands for the last four months.

I talked to Mowbray recently; he had just come back from a brief visit. He said the Duchess is expecting a child in September and they both appeared to be happy and content."

Addington continued to pull nervously at his lip. "Do you believe it?"

"No. A man like Dacre is just a coiled spring waiting to be released. But what else can we do?"

"Damn Dacre," said the Prime Minister for the second time. "His solution would be to give the Irish everything they want. Then, we'd have the Protestants arming against us. Arrest Lynch, I say. And any other of the leaders who are associated with him."

Portland rose to his feet, his flat face shining with sweat. "Just as you say, Mr. Prime Minister. I will communicate with Lord Hardwicke immediately."

And so it was on July 17 that Murdoch Lynch, for the second time in his thirty-seven years, found himself in jail. He was accompanied by Michael Walsh and Sean Molloy. John Farrell had escaped arrest by exiting through a window in the attic of the house in which he was staying and making his escape across the roofs. He was in hiding. Liam Emmet, who had been in the West, was still free.

Chapter Seventeen

Hearts with one purpose alone
Through summer and winter seem
Enchanted to a stone
To trouble the living stream.
                              —William Butler Yeats

George Mowbray had indeed been at Strands. He had been shooting in Scotland in early June and on his way home, impulsively, called in to see the Duke and Duchess of Dacre. It had been a perfectly delightful visit; both Christina and Dacre seemed rested and happy. Christina's skirts were fuller than they had been, but otherwise her beauty was more vivid than ever: Her skin glowed with a healthy golden color and there was the flush of wild rose in her cheeks. It was clear to Mowbray, as it was to anyone who came in contact with them, that the intensity of the bond between man and woman transcended the normal boundary of human relationships. It was a tangible thing, to be felt by anyone who strayed within their orbit.

Dacre appeared to be very busy. He and Mowbray had spent an evening in the Duke's study after Christina had retired, and Mowbray had seen for himself the work that Dacre was undertaking for the Royal Geographic Society. Dacre had discoursed lucidly and persuasively about the elevation of geography to a serious academic level, about the importance of mathematics, and the hilarious exploits of his neighbor, the mad squire; he had talked, in short, of everything except governmental affairs. Every effort Mowbray made to introduce politics met with a polite but definite rebuff. Finally, Mowbray had given up and allowed himself to be borne on the wit and charm of Dacre's conversation into other, less dangerous channels.

He found the same situation with Christina. They had a pleasant tea together one afternoon and she told him all about the translations she was doing of Irish sagas. "So much of Irish literature is oral," she said. "And unless someone writes it down, I am afraid it will be lost forever."

"You and Charles seem to be engaged in very scholarly activity," he said, watching her over his teacup and thinking she looked less like a scholar than anyone he knew. The June day brightened the room in which they sat, and limned the silver and gold beauty of the girl sitting in the big wing chair. She smiled at him. "The neighborhood is contagious," she said. "William Wordsworth and Samuel Coleridge, the authors of the *Lyrical Ballads*, are both living nearby, you know. Charles and Mr. Coleridge have had several long discussions on all kinds of trivial things, like Astronomy, Metallurgy, Chemistry, Geology, Medicine, Philosophy, et cetera, et cetera. Charles says he is a genius, and he well may be, but he is also very unhappy, poor man. I prefer Mr. Wordsworth, whose narrower interests more closely coincide with my own. And his sister is delightful."

Mowbray looked at the wide, grave brow of the Duchess of Dacre. "I wouldn't say your interests are narrow, Duchess," he said slowly.

"They were in the past," she answered somewhat grimly. "But they are changing," which was as close as either of them came to discussing the radical alteration in their way of life.

Mowbray stayed for four days. There were no clouds on the surface of life at Strands, and only someone who knew the principals well might feel a hint of uneasiness. They never talked about the future. And Christina never talked about the coming child. Dacre mentioned it once or twice, his face warm with pleasure, but Christina always let the topic die.

Perhaps, Mowbray thought, he was making a mountain out of a molehill. Perhaps they really were perfectly happy in their exile. But that it was an exile, even if voluntary, he was in no doubt at all.

In many ways, Christina was happy those spring months of 1801. She and Dacre were able to relax and share thoughts and interests that had been stifled by the thrust of the Emancipation campaign. As they walked in the garden, fished on sunny days in the lake, or lay wrapped in each others arms at night, the personal, the trivial, the fragments of their lives, which neither had ever shared with anyone else, were opened.

After dinner they would sit in the family drawing room with a fire to take away the chill of the spring evenings and play backgammon or chess or simply sit reading, occasionally exchanging some words about the book each was engrossed in.

Christina had started to work through Dacre's library, and discussions between them were envigorating and illuminating. Both brought to any topic minds of the first quality, but their very different thought processes made any exchange intriguing. Dacre's mind was relentlessly logical, lucid, and concise; Christina's worked with leaps of intuition; it was astonishing, Dacre said, how they so often ended up in the same place.

The torrent of their physical passion ran deeper than ever. Body and soul, they were so locked together that any distress, no matter how carefully camouflaged, was bound to be found out by the other. And there were hidden tensions.

Dacre was keeping a very close eye on Ireland and on the Government. Across the channel the Irish were burning, pillaging and rioting; Murdoch was drawing huge numbers of people to his rallies. Clearly any English Government must make up its mind to do something about Ireland. Either it must subdue her by force or try to win her by concession. As the Government delayed and delayed in making a move, Dacre was becoming more and more convinced that repression would be its answer to the problem posed by Ireland. And to Dacre, coercion unaccompanied by concession seemed an act of indefensible tyranny. As the spring moved into the summer, he found himself coming closer to the conscious recognition that he would have to act. He had hoped that the wisdom and the conscience of England's rulers would seek to lift Ireland out of all those injustices which could be directly traced to English misgovernment. He had been wrong. To win concessions, Ireland would have to fight.

Dacre's feelings about the situation in which he found himself were ambiguous. His tenure in Parliament had not been a comfortable one, but it had been what he had been bred for all his life. He had been brought up in the inner circles of Tory society and

171

when he had entered Government, reluctantly, he had declared himself a Tory also. By the time he entered Parliament, however, Dacre had lost any idealism he might once have had about party politics. He had a massive, well-trained mind whose scope was constantly circumscribed by the necessities of party discipline. He had often felt himself to be in a thoroughly false situation, but his only option lay in changing parties, and that hardly seemed a solution. The Whigs were chaotic and frustrated, condemned to perpetual opposition and held together only by the figure of Charles James Fox.

It was not satisfactory. But it was his world. It was vigorous and brilliant, luxurious and cultured. He could lead an Irish party in Parliament and still retain his ties to it; if he joined Murdoch Lynch in an open defiance of English law, he would not be forgiven.

Ireland was the hidden canker in their love; to survive they observed an unwritten law: It must not be mentioned. And through the bright, cloudless days of spring and summer, it lay like a stone in the midst of the stream of their love; submerged, yet around it the waters were troubled.

July was hot and Christina's habit was to lie down in the cool of her bedroom to rest after lunch each day. Dacre usually rode out on some estate business; often he would go for a swim in the lake. One afternoon a shower blew up and he returned earlier than usual. He went up to his dressing room to change his wet clothes, dismissed his valet, and quietly entered the bedroom.

Christina was asleep in the huge bed. Dacre looked for a moment at the spill of silver hair and smooth bare shoulder that protruded from the covers, then went to close the window as the rain was coming in. When he turned around she was awake.

"I'm sorry, love," he said contritely, going to kiss her. "I didn't mean to wake you."

She pushed her hair back and smiled. "It's all right, I should be getting up now anyway." Her fingers touched his bright hair, damp from the shower. "Did you get caught in the rain, Charles?"

"I did. I didn't mind it, but Falcon did. He bolted for the stable at the first drop." He looked at her, his eyes very gentle. "How are you feeling?"

Christina's eyes widened for a minute as she seemed to look inward. "I'm fine," she said, "and the baby is full of energy, too. He has been very active today."

He sat beside her on the bed and picked up her hand. "You always refer to the baby as 'he,'" he said, taking advantage of her rare willingness to talk on this subject. "Is that motherly instinct or wishful thinking?"

She smiled. "Both, I guess. I want a boy because I want to give you an heir. And I have a feeling I am going to get my wish."

He looked at her polished fingernails and sturdy, capable hand. "If it is a boy," he said slowly, "would you like to name him Niall?"

He felt her hand go rigid in his, and heard the harsh, shocked intake of her breath. "No!" she said violently, "No!" She pulled away from him, slipped out of bed, and went to stand by the window. He looked in distress at her slender back; he could hear the rapidness of her breathing. Then she turned toward him and the swelling of her stomach under her thin negligee was evident. When she spoke, her voice was tight with suppressed emotion. "Call him by an English name," she said. "That is what he will be."

There was an appalled silence as both looked with dawning horror at the rift their words had made in the veil that sheltered them from this truth they had determined to ignore. Dacre looked at the rigid face of his wife, his own features brutally composed. "You once told me," he said, disregarding even further the unwritten rule by which they lived, "that there is no prison in the world worse than love. Is that how it is?"

Pain was engraved on her face and sounded in the very timbre of her voice. "Oh my love. Without you there is only bitterness and drought. We are grappled to each other by hoops of steel; if our love is a prison, yet it is the only freedom I know."

His eyes, so densely green, never left her face. Finally he nodded slowly. "I know," he said in a tired voice. His hand reached out toward her, then dropped, and he walked to the door. "I'll be in my study," he said, and left the room.

Christina stood still, staring at the door that had closed so solidly behind him, and her tears fell unregarded. Presently, having washed and dried her face, she summoned her maid and dressed for dinner. When they met in the dining room, they were careful to talk about unexceptional topics. Such was the state of affairs at Strands when news of Murdoch Lynch's arrest arrived.

Chapter Eighteen

Know that when all words are said
And a man is fighting mad,
Something drops from eyes long blind,
He completes his partial mind
For an instant stands at ease,
Laughs aloud, his heart at peace.

                              —William Butler Yeats.

The news came to Dacre in a letter from George Mowbray. Even in the country, the Duke's mail was delivered early and it was his habit to spend an hour or so at his desk each morning to deal with it. He recognized Mowbray's writing and opened his letter first, and a muscle tightened in his jaw as he read it.

"My dear Charles, I was at Portland House for dinner last night and a piece of information came my way that I feel it is my duty to pass along to you. The Government has ordered the arrest of Murdoch Lynch.

Portland sent the order to Hardwicke this morning. I don't know if you want to do anything, but I thought I would...." Dacre stopped reading and put the letter down. With great control, he spoke to the portrait of one of his ancestors which hung on the wall. "The bloody fools," he said clearly. "The goddam, bloody fools."

He said nothing to Christina until after dinner. Outwardly, his day had not differed from any of those that preceded it. But under his disciplined demeanor, Dacre's relentlessly logical brain was evaluating the Government's move and his own options in the face of it. By dinnertime he had made his decision; a decision, he realized ruefully, that he had been moving toward for a long time.

Now that events were forcing him into action, Dacre felt as if a great weight had rolled off him. He sat down to dinner with Christina, more light-hearted than he had been for a long time. His mood was evidently infectious, for Christina too seemed merrier and more relaxed. They went into the drawing room after dinner, and Dacre closed the door behind him. He put Christina into the high wing chair that best supported her back, but he himself remained on his feet. He poked at the fire for a minute, for even in July the evenings were cool in the mountains, then turned, his hands still grasping the iron, and began to speak in a level voice.

"I heard from George Mowbray today, Christina. The Government has finally decided to act on Ireland. They have ordered the arrest of Murdoch Lynch."

All the color drained from Christina's face. "On what charge?" she said through stiff lips.

Dacre's smile was not pleasant. "The charge doesn't matter, since they do not plan to bring him to trial."

Christina's eyes were huge and dark, the only spot of color about her. "What can we do?" she whispered.

"Murdoch was on the right path, Christina. All of his activities were perfectly constitutional. He was in the process of organizing a vast political movement which no army could be called upon to suppress. The Government's action in arresting him is the measure of its fear." He paused, and the set of his mouth was decidedly grim. "But they won't arrest me; the Lords would never stand for it."

She stared at him soundlessly, then the color flooded back to her face. "What do you mean?" she said lightly.

"I mean to fight, little eagle," he said soberly. "Not with a gun; with something far more potent—the English constitution. Murdoch has raised the issue: Are the masses, well-organized but acting constitutionally, to be allowed to have their way? Murdoch and his fellow leaders have been suppressed, at least temporarily. It is for you and me, I think, to take up the fight for them."

Her face was perfectly still, schooled and expressionless. "I do not want you to do this for me," she said evenly. "We must be in this together, with whole hearts, or we must stay out of it."

Dacre's face was as calm as hers and his voice had its usual deep, even cadence, but there was about him a sense of suppressed energy that was new. "This is not a hasty decision on my part, Christina. It has been coming, I think, ever since we sat around a fire in the mountains of Kerry and you said to me, 'Do you know, Your Grace, what the land system is in Ireland?'" He smiled at her briefly. "Then Murdoch organized this Catholic Society. That was a stroke of genius, Christina. I never would have thought of it. It is the only way enough pressure, legal pressure, might be put on the Government, and the King, to force them to accept Emancipation."

A faint line had appeared between her level brows.

"I don't understand, Charles. The mass meetings and demonstrations are impressive, I grant you. But unless they move from peaceful assembly to armed hostility, I don't think the Government is going to change."

Dacre pulled a carved Chippendale chair over and sat down directly facing Christina. He leaned forward, his green eyes intent on her face. "I agree that the agitation must lead to some specific challenge, but that challenge does not have to be made in the field."

"Then where?"

"In Westminster. Ireland must go ahead and elect a Catholic to Parliament."

There was silence, then Christina began to laugh. "It is so simple, Charles. And no one ever thought of it." Her eyes suddenly narrowed. "How long have you had it in mind?"

"Since Murdoch first started holding his meetings." He met her scrupulously expressionless eyes and his mouth twisted. "I know, but I had to give the Government a chance to act."

"And they have."

He nodded grimly. "I never had much hope of their acting out of rightness. I did hope I might have thrown a scare into them."

"If they had any sense, they would have been scared," she said seriously as she considered the serene arrogance of his words. "But, Charles, who will run? And is it even legal for a Catholic to stand for Parliament? Won't he be suppressed from the start?"

"Oh it is perfectly legal for a Catholic to stand," he assured her. "The problem comes when he arrives at Westminster to take the oath of allegiance and supremacy. The words require him to swear that 'the sacrifice of the Mass and the invocation of the Virgin Mary and other saints, as now practiced in the Church of Rome, are infamous and idolatrous.' Clearly, no Catholic could agree to that."

178

"So, knowing this, an electorate who votes for a Catholic is making as strong a defiance of the political establishment as can constitutionally be made."

"Precisely. It should be done at a by-election, I think, so that the eyes of both islands are not distracted. One should be coming up within a few months; Lawton is not going to stay on for long."

"Who will run?" she repeated.

"That will be up to you, and to Murdoch. If Murdoch is released from jail, he would be ideal. But we have time to make that decision. The first thing is for me to pay a visit to Westminster." He smiled, looking suddenly very young. "I do not think they will be pleased to see me."

Once he had made his decision, Dacre moved quickly. In three days he was in London, arriving just days before Parliament recessed. There were about fifty members sitting in the Lords' Chamber when Dacre took his seat, and the sight of his bright head and sunburned, hawklike face caused the speaker to falter momentarily. Word of his presence circulated swiftly so that when he rose to speak the visitors benches were filled with members from the Commons, headed by the Prime Minister himself.

Effortlessly pitching his voice so it could be heard in the farthest reaches of the room Dacre began, "I should like, my lord, to address myself to the Government's arrest of the Irishman Murdoch Lynch and his colleagues." His words fell on dead silence and even the strongest nerves were vibrating by the time he finished. It was a bitter and serious speech, dealing with the centuries of injustice and division which the Act of Union had been designed to remedy. "What is it Murdoch Lynch wants for his countrymen, the Catholics of Ireland?" he concluded. "What is his crime? He wishes them to share in the blessings of the En-

179

glish constitution, to truly reap the political benefits promised by the union of our two countries. You charge him with intemperance in his exertions to win participation in the constitutional right of parliamentary representation, and you charge him at the same time with a design to overturn that same constitution which grants the right. If he desired to destroy it, my lord, would he seek to share it?"

There was scarcely the sound of breathing as the rulers of England watched one of their most brilliant, powerful, and inscrutable colleagues issue the most serious political challenge many had yet faced. "I find I cannot tolerate the blatant abrogation of constitutional rights this Government has indulged in. But the constitution, I believe, is greater than any single Government. I am going to recommend to the Irish people that they continue on their present course of action. I shall advise them to remain within the law and the constitution. Let them stand, even though they have to stand on the last plank of the constitution, let them stand until that plank is taken from under their feet."

Dacre's face was a sculpture in bronze as he left the floor of the chamber. He left behind him mingled feelings: anger, outrage, shame, bewilderment, but most of all, fear. For behind his challenge lay a threat: Any organization of the Irish masses in their terrible poverty and misery and their fierce resentment of their condition, had all the seeds of violent insurrection. If the demands of the Irish for constitutional reform were not met, the alternative could very well be civil war.

From London, Dacre went to Dublin, and in the chill dark of Kilmainham Gaol he met with Murdoch Lynch. The dark, damp room with its high barred windows looking on to a small dark courtyard put him forcibly in mind of Christina's imprisonment, and the face with which he greeted Murdoch was one the

Irishman had never seen before. The sight of Dacre was surprising enough, but the concentrated passion that marked his eyes and his mouth left Murdoch momentarily silent before him.

Dacre looked once again around the thick, damp walls and spoke grimly. "I will say to you, Murdoch Lynch, what I said to the English Parliament: The Government may temporarily circumvent the constitution, but in the end an appeal to the constitution will triumph over any Government or any King."

Murdoch's pale face looked thinner than ever, but his blue eyes were intense on Dacre's face. "Does this mean you are coming with us?" he asked bluntly.

"Yes," said Dacre, and his eyes met Murdoch's straightly. "All the way."

Murdoch wrote to Christina that night. After reporting on his interview with Dacre, he wrote in his clear, upright hand: "It is given to few men to soar high above the prejudices of race, class, and creed, and take a bold and far-seeing view of human action and its ultimate effect upon the human community. It is a gift of vision and of courage. I am glad that such a man is your husband."

Chapter Nineteen

Pallas Athene in that straight and arrogant
    head...

—William Butler Yeats

Before Dacre had reached Strands after his visit to
Ireland, the Government had taken action. Thirty-six
hours after Dacre's visit, Murdoch Lynch was released
from jail. It was done in the hopes of placating Dacre
and eviscerating any action he might be planning. It
came too late; Dacre was committed. And his actions,
ruthless, energetic, and thorough, were the relieved
response of a born fighter to a situation in which deeds
at last took precedence over prudence and caution.

Christina, too, had been busy. Dacre returned to
find trunks in the hall and a household seemingly in
the process of a major move. He found Christina in
the butler's pantry and the face she turned to him was
bright and pure as a candle's flame.

"Charles." She reached a hand up to touch his face. He caught her fingers in his and bent his head to kiss them.

Her lips curved, but she said merely, "You must be thirsty. Come to my sitting room and take some refreshment."

She turned to the major-domo, who said immediately, "I will send something immediately, Your Grace." She nodded and, linking her arm with Dacre's, led the way up the stairs.

Dacre followed her without a word and waited patiently as she closed the door and went to sit in the high-backed chair she had been using lately. He took his own usual seat and said quietly, "Well, little eagle?"

"We are going to Ireland, Charles," she said. "I can do nothing here, nor can you. It is imperative that we be visibly on the scene."

His voice was passionless and logical. "You cannot travel. You are seven months pregnant."

"I can if we go by sea. We can sail south and go directly to Kerry. The baby will be born at Clancarthy House in Killarney, the house where I was born." Her brow was wide and grave, her eyes a clear gray under the level brows. "It is not just a personal whim, Charles. It would be a move of enormous symbolic significance, one that would unite the Irish people behind us more surely than a hundred well-argued, intelligent speeches could ever do."

His first impulse was to forbid it; all his protective instincts were outraged at the thought of her undertaking such a journey. But as he looked at her face he saw again the wind-swept, treeless expanse of Slea Head and the girl riding to meet him, solitary and brave. All the courage, the pride, the tenacity, the resilience, the passion, which had made her such a force in British and Irish affairs were there in the lineaments of her face. And Christina knew the Irish people as no

183

one else did; her sense of what would move them had always been sure. The girl who had been willing to fast to death in the Tower of London knew better than anyone else the value of a symbolic action.

"Will you promise me not to exert yourself until after the baby is born?" he asked.

"Yes. And I have spoken with Dr. Santon; he approves of the trip by sea."

His eyes were very green in his tanned face as he smiled at her. "When do we leave?"

Her smile was mischievous, her eyes lit with laughter. "There is no point in sneaking home, like thieves in the night. I will write to Liam, and to Owen O'Neill, who is my agent in Kerry. Let us give them a week, at least, to adjust to the situation."

He shook his head ruefully. "A week, you mean, to organize a hero's welcome for you."

"Poor Charles," she said sympathetically. "You are going to be so uncomfortable. All your English restraint and reserve will be outraged. But we are not dealing with ideas of law or philosophic concepts in Ireland. We are dealing with people; poor, uneducated, oppressed people, who need something concrete to fight for. They need a leader, a deliverer, a Messiah. It is going to be very emotional." Her eyes, serious now, held his intently. "We are pledged to try to win necessary reforms for Ireland through legislation in Westminster, but there exists in the present situation a complex relationship between violence and constitutionalism. You know that."

She had brought out into the open the issue they had managed to dodge so efficiently during the first campaign for Emancipation. But Christina had meant what she said before he went to London; they were in it together, or not at all. And this time she was hiding nothing.

"I know that the leader of a mass movement on the

brink of revolution will receive a very serious hearing at Westminster," he answered dispassionately. "The threat of insurrection is the stick we must wield if we are to carry the legislation we want through Parliament. We are walking a very narrow line, Christina, between lawful and unlawful dissent. But with discipline and tenacity I believe we can win, *if* we keep just to the right side of the law."

She nodded so vigorously that a few strands of shining silver hair came loose from her chignon. "I believe we can too, Charles. The important thing now is to organize the Irish masses, a job Murdoch has begun brilliantly."

"Yes he has. And I think his plans and mine fit together very comfortably."

She pushed her loosened hair off her face and her eyes on his tanned and sculptured face were suddenly altered. "I missed you," she said quietly.

At that he rose and went to kneel beside her chair, his face against her breast, her cheek against his short, bright hair.

They sailed from Whitehaven on the Duke's yacht in early August. They went through the Irish Sea around the southern tip of Ireland past the main peninsulas of Cork and Kerry until they reached Dingle Bay. The weather was clear and the sea calm. Christina spent the day on deck and slept well at night; Dacre watched her carefully but no sign of discomfort or distress ever clouded the clear serenity of her face. As the *Viking Queen* passed the high, forbidding promontory of Slea Head, both Dacre and Christina were on deck, their eyes fixed on the grim fortress towering above the sleek yacht. She slipped her hand into his and their eyes met briefly. What passed between them did not need words.

They dropped anchor at Killorglin. The shore was

black with people. Gray clouds had moved in, dimming the brilliant sun they had had earlier, but nothing could dim the welcome that awaited the last of the MacCarthys as she returned to the land of her birth.

Dacre stood beside Christina on the deck of the yacht and watched a small boat rowing out to meet them. He recognized its occupant before she did. "It's Lynch," he said, his eyes on the slender, dark-haired man with whom he had, surprisingly, reached such understanding in a damp Kilmainham cell. It was Murdoch, and Liam Emmet and Michael Walsh as well as Owen O'Neill, Christina's agent. As the men climbed the ladder onto the boat's deck, Christina's eyes shone with pleasure. Dacre stood back a little and let her greet her vociferous band of countrymen; but Murdoch, after scrutinizing Christina carefully and kissing her lightly flushed cheek, came over to the Duke.

"There are easily ten thousand people," he told Dacre. "In Killorglin and along the route to Killarney. I have twenty men to ride escort around the carriage. The trip to Clancarthy House will probably take a few hours. I don't anticipate any trouble."

Dacre looked at his wife's glowing face and smiled ruefully. "Christina shouldn't have any trouble, either."

Murdoch's intense blue eyes were steady on the Duke's hawklike face. "Thank you," he said surprisingly.

Dacre didn't pretend not to understand. "I had no choice," he said.

The eyes of the tall English aristocrat and the slender Irish revolutionary both swung, irresistibly, to the silver-haired girl whose full green cloak partially disguised her advanced pregnancy. "I never thought you would," said Murdoch. And, unexpectedly and infectiously, Dacre began to laugh.

Christina heard him and turned to draw him into her circle. Briefly, Murdoch told her of his arrangements. There was amused sympathy in her eyes as she slipped her arm through her husband's. "At least this time you will be escorting me toward a happy destination, Charles."

"That thought will sustain me," he answered gravely.

As it was, the reception that awaited them on the shore and all along the miles to Killarney and Clancarthy House would remain vividly in Dacre's memory for the rest of his life. He sat next to Christina in the old-fashioned, open carriage Murdoch had procured, ready to order her to the floor at the first hint of trouble. None came. The crowds in the town and along the roadway had come for one reason only: to see Christina MacCarthy. They shouted, they cheered, they held their children high for a glimpse of Ireland's last chief come home to lead them once again into a new kind of battle. And not a few also craned to see the English Duke who had become her husband. Murdoch, riding beside the carriage, watched the Duke also and wondered what the Gaelic-speaking peasants who cheered him so enthusiastically made of this tall, fair-haired man with the sculptured face and green, watchful eyes.

For Christina, the ride was the culmination of months of hopes and plans. She was home. The sound of Gaelic in her ears, the sight of Carrauntoohil towering on her right, the sparkling water of Lough Leane before her; she was home. And Charles was with her. She turned and, finding his eyes on her, smiled. His returning smile said all she wanted to know and she touched his arm briefly, a gesture both graceful and strangely intimate. Murdoch, watching them, felt his chest tighten and resolutely turned his eyes to the crowd.

Clancarthy House was a surprise. Built of mellow brick, it was comfortable and gracious with none of

187

the medieval grandeur that distinguished Strands. "My father built it for my mother," Christina had told Dacre. "Kilmarrin Castle, which was for centuries the MacCarthy residence, had excellent qualifications as a fortress and virtually none as a home. My father thought the change from Letzau to Kerry would be violent enough, without subjecting my mother to Kilmarrin. We'll have to ride over one day to see it. Winds howl down the hallways and the walls drip."

"Does it have rats?"

"Of course."

"I can scarcely wait to see it," Dacre had said drily.

But he was pleasantly surprised by Clancarthy House. All of the MacCarthy tenants had lined the courtyard as they pulled in, and the cries of "MacCarthy More," had been loud and enthusiastic. Christina had spoken in Gaelic and Dacre had spoken a few words in English, then they were in the comfortable, many-windowed room that served as the drawing room of Clancarthy House. The windows looked over the lakes and mountains of Killarney, and Dacre, bred in one of the most beautiful sections of England, had to admit the view was breathtaking.

Christina's clear face was bright and pure as a flame. "Well, we have dropped the glove," she said. "The news of today's activities should alarm a few souls in London. But," she continued with the implacable clarity which always distinguished her judgment, "we always had Kerry behind us. We must not draw the same conclusions from today's demonstration as we hope the rest of the world will."

"Perhaps not, Christina, but do not underestimate it either. There is a tide swelling in our favor; it only remains for us to exploit it properly." The speaker was Murdoch, and his light eyes were unusually bright in his narrow, dark face.

"We will," said Liam Emmet, and his guarded eyes

glanced with reluctant admiration at Dacre. "Murdoch will run for Parliament. This time we will fight our battle in the open, with England's own law as our weapon."

Dacre sensed the veiled hostility behind Liam's wary brown eyes, and guessed also the reason for it. He gave the young man his rare, warm smile and said seriously, "You have done a magnificent job, all of you, in organizing the peasants of this country into what must rank as a political army. It is for us now to put an effective weapon into its hand: the legal and constitutional election of a Catholic to Parliament. But Murdoch must be elected and the kind of public show of solidarity we saw here today is invaluable in creating the disciplined defiance that we need."

Dacre's words, his use of Murdoch's first name, but most of all his smile broke through Liam's hostility and the reserve of Michael Walsh. The discussion of plans that followed was easy and unconstrained.

Christina, who knew how deliberate Dacre's charm could be and how cold-bloodedly he used it, regarded him skeptically when the others had gone. He met her wide gray eyes and the corners of his long mouth twitched irresistibly. "I meant every word I said, little eagle. But you must realize that I have a grave handicap to overcome in order to be accepted by your comrades."

"I know it. You are English."

After a moment of blank silence he began, disconcertingly, to laugh. "That wasn't what I was thinking of," he gasped when he could catch his breath. And, resolutely changing the subject, he refused to say more.

Chapter Twenty

Give to these children, new from the world,
Silence and love;
And the long dew-dropping hours of the night,
And the stars above.

—William Butler Yeats

They stayed at Clancarthy House for all of August
and September. Dacre made several short trips, twice
to Dublin, once to Clare and once to Cork, but otherwise he stayed in Killarney, waiting, with Christina,
for their child to be born. Christina rarely went beyond
the confines of the grounds, as excessive walking tired
her and the jolting of a carriage was uncomfortable;
but she encouraged Dacre to ride out on his own and
in doing so, he became acquainted with two important
sides of Irish life.

The first thing that impressed him was the beauty

of the countryside. Killarney was magnificent: There were flowering groves and dells filled with thorn trees and rose-colored briars and wild rhododendrons; there were ravines and wooded cliffs covered with wild roses and brimming with dragonflies; there were deep woods splashed with sunshine and, everywhere one looked, the mountains, jagged and towering, hard as the life they guarded.

For there was another side to the Kerry he saw: the life of the people. Once he left the MacCarthy lands, the living standard of the peasants changed drastically and the stunning beauty of the landscape stood in cruel contrast to the lot of the people who dwelt there. The reality of that Kerry was hard and brutal: the reality of mud-walled cabins, bare-footed peasants, a whole bitter struggle for existence. During those weeks, while he was waiting for his child to be born, Charles Standish discovered for himself the Ireland hidden from those of his class. He saw the huts made of earthen sod, or of mud and straw; he smelled the rank reek of the wet turf on the fires; he felt the rain on his neck as it dripped through the thatch; his eyes smarted with the smoke and the damp as men, women, children, and animals all crowded for shelter into the one room. And everywhere he went he was constantly surprised by the unfailing politeness and generosity of these same downtrodden people. All of the passion that Dacre was to unleash with such effectiveness in his future campaigns for land reform in Ireland had as its origin these weeks in Kerry.

Christina and Dacre were playing chess on the evening of September 12. They were seated in the comfortable sitting room that adjoined their bedroom and Christina was losing. She frowned suddenly at the board and moved her rook in order to protect her

191

queen. Dacre moved his knight. "Checkmate," he said quietly.

A brief smile crossed her face, then she sat perfectly still. Raising her eyes to him, she said, "I think it is time to send for Dr. Walsh."

He was beside her in a minute. "I thought there was something wrong. Let me take you inside."

She allowed him to walk her to the bedroom, where she lay down on the high wide bed. "The pains started this afternoon," she told him. "But they are coming faster and harder now."

"Christ, Christina! Why didn't you say something sooner. I'll send Matty for the doctor."

"No, go yourself, Charles."

He looked at her worriedly. "I shall be all right. Send Maureen to me. But go now."

He nodded and disappeared, happy, she knew, to be doing something at this, the most helpless time in a man's life.

He was back with the doctor in half an hour. Then, for the remainder of the night, Dacre sat in the sitting room, sweating and praying, as effectively exiled from the drama that was taking place in the bedroom as if he had been in China. Periodically the doctor appeared to assure him that all was going well. At one point, contrary to orders and to propriety, Dacre entered the bedroom to assure himself that Christina was indeed still alive.

Maureen had braided her thick fair hair, but tendrils had escaped from their confinement and clung to her cheeks and neck. She was very pale. But she smiled at him reassuringly. "He is putting up quite a battle, Charles, but I am winning." He bent to kiss her sweaty forehead and saw her face begin to stiffen with pain. He took her hand and felt his fingers would break within the vise of her grasp. The pain passed and Christina looked up into his face, paler now than

192

hers. "Dear God, Christina, is there anything I can do?"

"It is worse for you than it is for me," she told him, and meant it. "There is nothing for you to do but wait. I shall be all right." Then, as the pain washed over her again, she clenched her teeth. "Go," she said. And he went.

Niall Charles Fergus Standish, Viscount Borrow and future Duke of Dacre, was born as the dawn was breaking over Mangerton Mountain on the morning of September 13. The news of his coming rang across Ireland as if this birth was a pledge of renewal and regeneration for the whole of the country. The greatness of England and Ireland had combined to produce this child; surely they would create new life for the land of his birth as well. So the pubs were filled, and families gathered to celebrate, and clergy offered prayers and masses.

The joy at Clancarthy House was quieter, but deeper. For perhaps the first time since the death of her father, Christina truly forgot politics. Ironically, as the country celebrated its sudden belief in a future deliverance, Christina lost herself in the profoundly personal love of husband and of child. Watching Dacre with his golden-headed son, so astonishingly comfortable and natural with the tiny baby, Christina felt tears cloud her eyes and constrict her throat. But when he turned to her, as he always did, the warm glow of love on her face effectively hid the tears.

For over three months Dacre had been unfailingly gentle and tender with his wife. Her advanced pregnancy and fragility after childbirth had stirred a profoundly protective instinct in him; passion was muted and softened into a love totally undemanding and content to rest merely in her physical presence. This change in their relationship had seemed as natural to Christina as breathing, and she inhaled his careful love as freely as the air.

The intensity of her feelings for her child surprised her. Her emotions during pregnancy had not been deeply maternal; in fact, she tended to look upon the baby's birth as something to get through and over with, so she could get on with the important business of her life. But when she felt his silky head under her cheek, and the warm weight of him against her breast, such love welled up within her that she almost forgot to breathe. Dacre, whose delight in his son was perfectly genuine, was drawn within the warm maternal cocoon of her love. But during that first month after Niall's birth, Christina's world was her baby. As he watched her shining, silvery head bent over the cradle, Dacre's mouth took on a distinctly wry expression. What he had been unable to do, what the entire British Government had been unable to do, had been accomplished very effectively by one seven-pound baby boy.

But the purely emotional cloud Christina had immersed herself in could not last forever. The talk of visitors: Murdoch and Liam and the Bishop of Kerry, who baptized Niall, seemed to wash over her, but she missed very little of what was said. She began to do a great deal of walking, then riding, and her body firmed up to its normal healthy slenderness. She felt energetic for the first time in months.

Dacre had been to Dublin twice since Niall's birth, and it was a rainy, chilly late November day that Christina looked out on as she awaited his return from the second of those visits. He had been gone a week, and she had found herself increasingly restless as the days of his absence went on. Even the baby failed to occupy her completely, and she wandered about the house, touching Dacre's books and his clothes and looking out the window toward the east.

The downpour caught Dacre about six miles from home. He had traveled in an open carriage despite the weather, so he was thoroughly soaked by the time he reached Clancarthy House. Christina met him at the door and shook her head ruefully at his streaming hair and sodden clothes. She reached up to touch his cheek and he bent to kiss her. Both cheek and lips were wet and chill. "You're frozen, Charles," she said. "There's a fire in the bedroom. Go on up and I'll bring you a brandy."

His green eyes flickered under their long, wet lashes, but he said only, "Good idea, love; I am cold."

As she was coming upstairs with a tray, Christina passed Dacre's valet in the hall. He was carrying a pair of wet boots and, from the look on his face, Christina knew that he had been dismissed. She continued along the passage and quietly opened their bedroom door.

Dacre was standing in front of the fire, with only a towel wrapped around his waist. He had evidently rubbed his hair, for it was starting to brighten and feather at the ends. She stood silent for a moment, watching the way the strong column of his neck merged into the powerful, smoothly-muscled shoulders and back. Something, dead within her these last few months, stirred and woke. She had been silent, but he sensed her presence and turned to face her. Slowly she put her tray down on a small, mahogany table and walked to meet him. Her breath was coming short and hard, and his eyes, as she looked at him, were narrow with passion.

"I've missed you," he said, his deep voice deeper than usual.

She reached up to touch his strong, smooth chest. "It has been a long time," she answered. And then

195

they were in each other's arms, the passion between them urgent, intense, desperate; their need too great for nuances.

They were two hours late for dinner that evening and, whatever the servants may have thought, no one said a word.

Chapter Twenty-One

We Irish, born into that ancient sect
But thrown upon this filthy modern tide
And by its formless spawning fury wrecked,
Climb to our proper dark....
                                    —William Butler Yeats

During the months of early autumn, it was Dacre who worked with Murdoch to organize the Emancipation campaign. Their ultimate challenge, that of running Murdoch for the next vacant Irish seat in the House of Commons, was known to only a few. But there was little doubt in the minds of Dublin Castle or of the Government in Westminster that Murdoch Lynch and the Duke of Dacre had some scheme in mind. Whether or not that scheme involved violence was the question that plagued them.

Murdoch's job was to continue the organization of the people on a grass-roots level. The fact that he had the active support of the Catholic priesthood and of many of the bishops was an enormous aid. At the various meetings he held around the country, to speak on the importance of Emancipation, the only thing more worrisome to the Government than the size of the crowds he drew was the disciplined order that prevailed. An Irish people united and controlled was an ominous spectacle, and the British Government, seized with something near panic, began to send more troops into the country.

Dacre's job was to deal with the Government. In a serious conversation with the Executive Board of the Catholic Society, Dacre had stated his operating principle. To the question, "How far will the Government go?" put by Michael Walsh, Dacre had answered: "It will do what we can make it do, so long as we stay on the right side of treason." And it was this tenet that he had fixed in mind as he dealt with the officials at Dublin Castle and, through them, with Westminster.

Murdoch's Catholic Society and the increasingly organized peasant movement was alarming enough to the Government. But what really seriously frightened them was Dacre. With that typically English sense of inborn superiority, Westminster had always felt it could, if necessary, deal with the unruly Irish. But never before had a great English aristocrat put his power and his talent at the service of the Irish peasant. "I am afraid of him because I don't know what he is up to," wrote the Irish chief secretary to Home Secretary Portland. And Prime Minister Addington wrote to Lord Lieutenant Hardwicke bitterly, "We are in the happy state in Ireland that it depends upon the prudence and discretion of Dacre and the leader of the Catholic Society whether we shall have a rebellion there or not in the next few months."

Violent rebellion was Dacre's bargaining card, and he played it skillfully. Delicately irritating the Government's fears, he gently pointed out the explosive situation simmering in Ireland. But for Murdoch Lynch, Liam Emmet, and others, whom Dacre had persuaded to follow the path of constitutionalism, violence would certainly gain the upper hand, he suggested to the Lord Lieutenant regretfully. And in thus drawing attention to the threat he was averting, he uttered a sort of threat himself. The Government poured more troops into the country and began to have serious doubts about the reliability of Irish troops stationed abroad.

So matters stood when Gerald Fitzsimons, a member of Parliament for County Clare, died suddenly in his London home one Sunday evening. A seat for the House of Commons was thus available, and a special election called.

There appeared to be little doubt as to the outcome of the election. The Fitzsimons family had held the seat for years and the son of Gerald Fitzsimons was prepared to stand for his father's place. The family had always shown themselves to be sympathetic to the peasants and were known as good landlords. The election, the Government thought, was a mere formality.

On October 29 the Catholic Society formally announced that it intended to run Murdoch Lynch for the Clare seat. The news electrified Ireland. It horrified Westminster.

Lord Hardwicke, Ireland's Lord Lieutenant, sent an urgent message to Dacre; Dacre, with Christina and Murdoch, was in Ennis, the county town of Clare from which the election was to be held, organizing Murdoch's two-week campaign.

The issue was very simple: Would the peasants of County Clare defy their landlords, who for generations had considered their tenants' votes as part of their personal property, risk eviction, and vote for Murdoch Lynch and Catholic Emancipation? Balloting was held in public and the landlord often escorted his tenants

199

to the polling place and then stood by to make sure everyone voted as instructed. Would the peasants have the courage to cross over and vote for Murdoch?

Their campaign plan was also simple: In those two weeks Christina, Murdoch, and the other leaders of the Catholic Society would travel every mile of the constituency and hold as many meetings and see as many people as possible. And from their pulpits the priests of Clare would preach a crusade to end for all time the political shackles placed by England on the Catholic people of Ireland. For the first time in history the native leaders and priests of the Irish people united to ask the wretched poor of the nation to act against their landlords.

Dacre went to one meeting with Christina before he left for Dublin to see Hardwicke. It was held at Clarecastle and about three hundred people were in attendance. The format they used that day was their format for the following two weeks. There was a platform put up in the open air and on it sat Murdoch, Christina, Liam Emmet, and John Farrell. The meeting was opened by the local parish priest, who led them all in a prayer. "We know, Oh Lord, what is the right thing for us to do. We pray for Your Grace to give us the strength and the courage to act as we ought. In the name of the Father and of the Son and of the Holy Ghost, Amen." He raised his eyes to look at his people and said simply, "My brothers and sisters in Christ, I am proud to introduce to you Lady Christina MacCarthy, now the Duchess of Dacre."

Dacre, standing at the back of the crowd, was prepared for loud cheering, but, as always, the volume of noise took him by surprise. The voices rent the heavens and washed over the slender, poised figure of the girl standing before them in deafening waves of sound. Finally, she raised her hand for quiet and, obediently, the crowd fell silent.

"I am here today to ask you to vote for Murdoch Lynch for Parliament," she said, in her clear, pure voice, perfectly audible to Dacre at the edge of the crowd. "The Irish Catholic today is an outcast in his own country. Nowhere in the western world is there a peasantry more destitute than here in Ireland. There is only one way to correct the ancient injustices of our land system, only one way in which we can give the soil of Ireland back to the people of Ireland: We must win political equality in Parliament. A victory for Murdoch Lynch is our way of saying to the lords in London: We want to work with you for the improvement of our people; we want a chance to peacefully better the living conditions of all Irishmen; we do not want to have to resort to the hillside again."

The corners of Dacre's long mouth quivered as he listened to her. He thought he would delay another day before going to Dublin, and give a chance for the news of Christina's speech to reach the Lord Lieutenant. All he could do with Hardwicke was bluff, leaving the Government to wonder whether or not he was as opposed to violence as he maintained. The veiled threat in Christina's remark about returning to the hillside would only add to the Government's mounting fears.

Murdoch's standard speech ran along lines similar to Christina's, and the reaction they got in Clarecastle was repeated in town after town. It was as if to the ignorant, downtrodden, and hungry masses of the Irish people a new Moses had arisen. Dacre, talking to a nearly hysterical Lord Hardwicke, had all the advantage of a revolution behind him which the Government was fully aware of but incapable of dealing with because it had not yet broken out.

The election was to be held on Tuesday, November 11. Dacre and Christina spent the night of November 10 at the Royal Hotel in Ennis. They got little sleep.

Murdoch, Liam, Michael Walsh, and John Farrell, who were also staying at the Royal, sat up with the Duke and Duchess until two in the morning, reluctant to leave the support of each other's company. In the midst of the tension they shared, Christina had time to reflect on Dacre's obvious acceptance by the other men, and his own naturalness in his present surroundings. He was their lifeline to the Government in Westminster, and they all recognized now that they needed him. But it was more than that: These tough patriots, veterans of rebellion and imprisonment, trusted the English Duke who had so miraculously taken up their cause. At one point in the evening, Liam went to the window to look out at the quiet street, then turned to say something. Dacre's deep voice answered and there was sudden laughter in the room, the laughter of people totally in tune with each other.

Finally Dacre caught Christina's eye and she rose. He stood too. "Well, gentleman, we will see you in the morning." There was a murmur of good nights and the eyes of the men in the room followed the fair heads of the Duke and Duchess of Dacre as they left the lounge.

Once they reached their bedroom Christina, like Liam, went compulsively to the window to stare out at the empty town, as if an answer to her question would be whispering in the night air of Ennis.

Dacre watched her straight back, compassion in his eyes. No matter how intensely involved he was in any issue, he retained always the ability to back away emotionally and see things objectively. The only time this precious objectivity had failed him was in his dealings with Christina; with her, reason and emotion were so entangled that he was never able to separate one from the other. But in all other matters he was able to maintain an icy clarity of thought; the very real passion and outrage he felt he kept harnessed for deliberate unleashing when it would prove most effective.

For Christina, thought and feeling were one totality; the flow of her logic fed upon the intensity of her passions. This difference between them made Christina the most effective speaker ever to address the Irish people and gave Dacre the edge he always held in Parliament, where life was governed by a multitude of rules, written and unwritten.

But, because of her temperament, Christina was suffering more now, and Dacre regarded her with a mixture of love and pity. There was a large upholstered rocking chair in front of the fire and he went and picked her up, then sat down in it with her in his lap. He could feel the tautness of her as she lay against him, so he cradled her gently and rocked slowly, his lips buried in the silver hair which covered her ear. He murmured comforting things to her, much as he did to his infant son, and gradually he felt her relaxing, warm and heavy against him. Then he carried her to the great four-postered bed, undressed her, and made love to her. At last, her head pillowed on his shoulder, she fell asleep.

Dacre, the rationalist, lay awake until the grayness of dawn began to creep into the room.

They started coming into town at seven in the morning. The polling place was in the small Ennis Town Hall, and there were two tables set up, one for John Fitzsimons and one for Murdoch Lynch. In front of all present, the voter had to approach the table of the candidate of his choice and cast his ballot.

The townsfolk had been voting since six, and the balloting was about evenly divided. At seven the first contingent from the outlying districts of Ennis came in. Father Sean O'Connor, who had implored his flock at mass yesterday to vote for their God and not for their landlord, led fifty men from his parish to the town hall. All fifty voted for Murdoch Lynch.

Christina, Dacre, Murdoch, and the others were at breakfast when they heard the news, and Liam crowed with delight. It was Christina who said, though her gray eyes shone, "We can't rely too much on the Holy Trinity vote. We were fairly sure we had that. It is the people from Inagh and Quin, who have always been escorted by their landlords, whom we need."

There was a large Protestant settlement at Clarecastle, and the vote from there was split, with the edge going to Fitzsimons. Encouraging to Dacre, however, was the fact that 75 percent of the Catholics voted for Murdoch.

The test came at about three in the afternoon. Murdoch was running ahead, but the tenants of the large landlords of Inagh and Quin had not yet voted. Christina, Dacre, and Murdoch were seated on the balcony outside the hotel's dining room when a young boy came galloping up the street. "They're coming!" he called to them. "The tenants from Quin! And Sir Henry is with them." Christina's hand on the arm of her chair tightened until the knuckles whitened. Sir Henry Tallant was one of the greatest landlords in the district. He was not an easy man. Evictions on his property were always high.

Into the streets of Ennis the tenants of Quin came, Sir Henry and his agent, Frank Morrow, riding behind them. The faces of the two men on horseback were grim; the men on foot looked sullen and downcast. "Poor devils," said Dacre, as he watched them come. "Driven to cast their votes, like cattle to market."

As the slow-moving crowd approached the balcony on which she stood, Christina moved to stand at the railing. The sun, hidden behind gray clouds all day, chose that moment to break out, glinting palely on her silvery hair, wide, grave brow, and darkened eyes. She said nothing, but raised a hand in greeting. Suddenly, from the center of the throng, came a voice, "Mac-Carthy More!" it cried, ringing and proud. And "MacCarthy More!" and "Catholics for Parliament!" and "Murdoch, boy, we're with you!" burst from the ranks as though a dam had broken. Under the angry, incredulous eyes of Sir Henry Tallant, his tenants poured to the polls to cast their votes for Murdoch Lynch and Catholic Emancipation.

They remained on the balcony until the polls closed at ten o'clock, but long before that the result was clear. The final tally made it official: 2,057 votes for Murdoch Lynch; 982 for John Fitzsimons. With a courage their leaders had hardly dared to hope for, the peasants of County Clare had stood up to be counted.

Chapter Twenty-Two

Sing the lords and ladies gay
That were beaten into the clay
Through seven heroic centuries;
Cast your mind on other days
That we in coming days may be
Still the indomitable Irishry.
                    —William Butler Yeats

Immediately after the election, Ireland erupted into parades and demonstrations, all conducted with a disciplined order that struck terror into the English authorities. Dacre left Ireland to discuss the Irish situation with a very receptive Government.

"No man can contemplate without alarm what is to happen in this wretched country," wrote the Lord Lieutenant of Ireland to the Home Secretary of England.

"No one can answer for the consequences of delay," the Home Secretary reported to the Prime Minister.

"We are no longer in the region of reform, we are in the very crisis of revolution," Dacre told the grim-faced Cabinet ministers he met with.

"The only alternative to Emancipation is civil war," wrote Prime Minister Addington to His Majesty at Windsor.

When Dacre returned to Ireland, a Catholic Emancipation Bill, similar to the one the King had rejected a year ago, was being drawn up by the Government.

When Parliament opened in January, Christina accompanied Dacre to London. They left the new Viscount Borrow, four months old, at Clancarthy House in the charge of his nurse; even Christina rejected the idea of taking him across the Irish Sea in midwinter.

Their arrival was quiet, but as soon as Dacre's tall figure appeared in the Lobby at Westminster, tension began to build.

The news of Christina's presence was spread by George Mowbray, who had it from Dacre. Soon a steady stream of visitors was arriving at the doorstep of Dacre House, led by Lord Henry Chatsworth and the rest of the Four Horsemen.

The Emancipation issue was out in the open, and the sides were lining up. On one side was the Government, backed by the brilliant and powerful Duke of Dacre. On the other was the Church of England, which was exerting itself to rally as much support in the House of Lords as it possibly could.

The House of Commons passed the Bill on February 2. On the evening of February 8, the Duke of Portland, Home Minister of His Majesty's Government, rose to introduce the Bill in the House of Lords. His speech was hardly calculated to appease the outraged churchmen. Fear alone, he made it clear, was the reason for this concession: "There is only one alternative to Emancipation, my lords," he said, "and that is civil war. This is the measure to which we must have looked, these are the means which we must have applied, if we had not embraced the option of bringing forward this measure."

Dacre sat listening to Portland with a thoughtful look in his veiled green eyes. He had carefully calculated the votes in his mind, and the number he could count on was not going to be enough to carry the Bill unless he could sway some of the unknowns and undecideds. As he listened to Portland he looked around the chamber, his eyes occasionally lingering on a face. By the time the Duke had sat down, Dacre had come to some conclusions about the men he would be able to appeal to.

After Portland, several other Government members rose to urge the Bill, each one emphasizing the precarious state of law in Ireland. Then Lord John George Beresford, Archbishop of Armagh and leader of the Church of Ireland opposition, took the floor. It was nearly midnight, and Beresford's eyes briefly met Dacre's across the room as he moved to adjourn. Dacre's face was serene as he walked out with the Earl of Plymstock. He nodded briefly to the Archbishop as he left the hall; both men knew the real test would come during the next day's debate, when they each would speak.

"I don't know how it will conclude, little eagle. The House of Lords hasn't had attendance as high as this in many years. Both the Government and the Church have been pressuring every peer they think will vote with them into attending. There are just too many unknown quantities for me to hazard a judgment."

They had finished dinner and Dacre was preparing to leave for Westminster. Christina was going also, but she was waiting for Lord Henry to escort her. She smiled at her husband, her eyes clear and unsha-dowed. "Whatever happens, I love you."

His long, slender fingers lightly touched her silvery head. "I know, Christina," he said soberly. "Thank God."

The House of Lords was filled to capacity when Christina arrived with Lord Henry. All the eyes in the visitor's gallery, as well as many on the floor, watched her as she took her place in the seat Dacre had reserved for her. She looked beautiful in a deep, forest-green velvet cloak, its hood pushed back off her pale, simply-dressed hair. The flawless gravity of her face was bro-ken momentarily by a smile as she saw Dacre watching her, but otherwise she sat quiet and still, intent on the debate.

When his lordship, the Archbishop of Armagh, rose to speak, the silence in the packed chamber was thick and absolute. In his person and in his position, Lord John George Beresford represented the strongest tra-ditions of the Protestant Ascendancy. He spoke, too, of fear; not the fear of civil war, but the ancient, deep-rooted fear of Rome. His voice rang around the cham-ber in solemn warning. This Bill of Catholic Eman-cipation, he intoned, was only the beginning of a pro-cess that would see the power in Ireland irrevocably transferred from one religion to another. He concluded in measured tones: "Are you prepared, my lords, to go to the lengths to which you will be urged, after you have conceded all that is now demanded? Are you prepared to sacrifice the Irish Church establishment and the Protestant institutions connected with it—to efface the Protestant character of the Irish portion of the Empire—to transfer from Protestants to Roman Catholics the ascendancy of Ireland?"

The silence in the House of Lords was tight with tension as the Archbishop sat down and the Duke of Dacre rose to reply to him. The light shone upon Dacre's burnished head and narrowed green eyes, glinting with temper and impatience. His deep voice was professionally pitched to reach the entire chamber:

"My lords, just over a year ago the Irish nation, by action of this Parliament, was joined to us in an Act of Union, making of our two nations one United Kingdom. We have met here tonight to decide on the future of that Union."

His eyes met those of Lord Beresford as he continued, "There are two ways only of dealing with Ireland at this juncture. We can extend to all the people of Ireland the rights and privileges which Protestant Irishmen have so proudly insisted on for themselves, and so govern the country through the public mind of the country. Or, we can move massive numbers of troops into Ireland and govern by martial law. Those are our choices."

With all eyes riveted upon him, Dacre laced his long fingers together and regarded his upturned palms. The edge of temper in his voice had disappeared and his deep, clipped tones were now sober and deliberately uninflected. "Eighty percent of the Irish people are Roman Catholic. They have remained Roman Catholic through centuries of oppression, through the horrors of famine and of the penal code. They are not likely to change because the Archbishop of Armagh does not approve of them."

And now, cold and calculated, Dacre unleashed his anger. "Are the Christian virtues of justice and charity quite beyond us in this land? Are the leaders of the Irish and the English Church so jealous of their power that they will refuse to admit a whole nation into political equality because it worships the same God in a slightly different manner? Are we to bar Murdoch Lynch from sitting in this Parliament in the name of the God who bade us to love our neighbor as ourselves?"

210

Into the silence, Dacre spoke gently. "My lords, you have been asked to pass this Bill out of fear. I ask you now to pass it out of justice. I am an Englishman and my pride in my country has always been based on her great tradition of representative government. The tyrant has never flourished on English soil. But if we deny to the Catholic people of Ireland their right to be represented in this body, then we deny the long tradition of representative government that started with Magna Carta. If we garrison Ireland the way we will be forced to if this Bill is defeated, then we will indeed become the tyrant. And tyranny, as the recent revolutions in America and in France have shown us, breeds its own destruction."

Dacre's eyes moved now slowly around the chamber, resting on the intent faces of his fellow peers. "Are the lords of England capable of seeing beyond the rhetoric of fear and of hatred and deciding this issue with statesmanship and with justice? And if not, then who is to lead us in the wilderness into which we shall all, Catholic and Protestant, English and Irish, be plunged by our failure tonight?"

There was continued silence for perhaps ten seconds after Dacre sat down, then the Lord Chancellor collected himself and asked for any further debate. Lord Henry turned to Christina and found her staring at Dacre, her face such a mirror of her private thoughts that he had to turn away, the corners of his mouth tight with pain.

There were several more speeches after Dacre's, but, as everyone knew, to all intents and purposes the debate was over. The only question that remained was: Who would prevail, Lord John George Beresford or Charles Standish?

The vote came at two in the morning. More peers voted on this bill than on any other in recent memory. The Churchmen held strong and, with the exception of the Bishop of Oxford, voted against Emancipation. But a sufficient number of England's nobles rose to Dacre's call, and the Catholic Emancipation Bill passed the House of Lords by a small majority.

It was April before the Emancipation chapter of Irish history was completed. In April, George the Third, angry and resentful, signed the Catholic Emancipation Bill into law.

On May 2, Murdoch Lynch, the first Catholic since the Reformation to do so, took his seat in the House of Commons. Dacre was present in the Peer's Gallery to watch him take the new oath of allegiance, and his still, powerful figure formed a disturbing backdrop to Murdoch's quiet, measured voice. A new era had opened in the ancient conflict between Ireland and England, and many of those present were uneasily aware that, with Dacre, an advantage had passed to the Irish side.

By the middle of May, Dacre had rejoined Christina in Kerry. The baby was flourishing and plans were underway to contest every vacant Irish seat with a Catholic candidate. They planned to be in London for the closing of Parliament, then to spend some months at Strands.

They sat one rainy evening in the lovely drawing room of Clancarthy House, comfortably silent, listening to the sound of the rain drumming against the windows.

"I am so happy, Charles," Christina said softly. "When I think of how unhappy I was a year ago, it does not seem possible."

He had been thinking much the same thing, but looked at her without surprise. They so often anticipated each other's feelings. "I know, little eagle. It has not been an easy path. And there is a rough road still ahead. But we know, now, what we can ask of each other."

Her eyes were dark as smoke as she thought back over the past two years. Then she picked up his hands and held them, palm up, on her own. With her eyes on their slender strength, she said matter-of-factly, "You hold more than my heart, Charles. You have my soul as well." She looked up and met his open green eyes. "Thank God it was you."

He knew what was in her mind: the agony of torn allegiance, the rawness of what she had seen as desertion and betrayal. There came, unbidden to his mind, the memory of that painful night when he had tried to force the love that was his as a gift. He heard again her aching voice: "There is no prison in the world that is worse than love."

He closed his hands on hers and spoke to her with quiet soberness. "I cannot guarantee that we will never be at odds again over what is the best path to follow for Ireland. But this I know, what we both want is peace and justice for all our people. Surely that is a goal we can pursue in honor and in quiet mind."

"It is a task worth the rest of our lives, and our children's as well," she answered. "Sometimes, though," she said huskily, "I wish we were just the two of us, alone together in some quiet place...."

The deep tones of desire darkened his voice as he watched the smooth white skin at the nape of her bent neck. "When you look at me like that," he murmured, "we are always alone." He kissed her neck and she melted against him. "My love, oh my love...."

A short time later the butler carried a tea tray to the drawing room only to find the door closed and locked. He tried it once again, then listened briefly at the door before going away again, a gentle smile on his face. He returned his tray to the kitchen and reported that Their Graces would not be requiring evening tea tonight.

About the Author

Joan Wolf is a native of New York City who presently resides in Milford, Connecticut, with her husband and two young children. She taught high school English in New York for nine years and took up writing when she retired to rear a family.

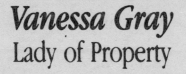